Y0-EGE-890

FIC
FER

Ferris, Jean.

2404

The stainless-steel
rule.

$11.01

DATE DUE	BORROWER'S NAME	ROOM NO.

FIC
FER

Ferris, Jean.

2404

The stainless-steel
rule.

**ALTERNATE LEARNING CENTER
LUCAS COUNTY OFFICE EDUCATION**

674004   04491B

THE STAINLESS STEEL RULE

Also by Jean Ferris

AMEN, MOSES GARDENIA

FARRAR STRAUS GIROUX / NEW YORK

Jean Ferris

THE
STAINLESS
STEEL
RULE

Copyright © 1986 by Jean Ferris
All rights reserved
Published simultaneously in Canada by Collins Publishers, Toronto
Library of Congress catalog card number: 85–45731
Printed in the United States of America
Designed by Claudia Carlson
First edition, 1986
Second printing, 1987

For my friends in the classes of 1982–1986
of University of San Diego High School

THE STAINLESS STEEL RULE

1

It was still dark when Fran picked me up at ten to six, the first Monday in October. I'd been standing on the sidewalk waiting for her for five minutes. I was always ready early for the first morning workout but never for any of the subsequent ones. The novelty of having to be in the pool by six wore off quickly, even though we only did it twice a week. The best part of morning workouts had always been that Fran and Mary and I did them together. Now it was just Fran and me. Of course, we'd known that's how it would be, since Mary was a year ahead of us in school and graduated before we did.

"Remember this Monday last year?" I asked Fran. I couldn't help it.

She looked at me and then turned back to her driving without answering. Of course she remembered.

. . .

A year ago. In the still, near-dawn darkness, we hurtled up the hill to the pool in Mary's little green car: Quasimotor, the Hatchback of Las Piedras High. The car was a seventeenth-birthday gift from Mr. and Mrs. Foster, Mary's foster parents. Mrs. Foster jokes that their name is the reason they decided to become foster parents. They'd had Mary for nine years, ever since her real parents abandoned her, and they loved her. Who wouldn't? Mary was beautiful, smart, talented—the kind of girl it's easy for us ordinary people to hate—but Mary was so nice you couldn't.

Mary was eating a whole-wheat brownie while she drove. I consider that a contradiction in purpose. I know everything there is to know about brownies, and they are supposed to be delectable and extravagant and even slightly wicked. If you make them nutritious and healthful, you have removed their essence. It's like the Heisenberg Uncertainty Principle we learned in chemistry sophomore year. If it's so uncertain, how come it gets the status of being a principle?

Anyway, Mary was eating her brownie, Fran was trying to sleep, her head bumping against the window, and I was making a halfhearted effort to finish my geometry. But it's hard to draw straight lines in a moving car.

Mary wheeled into our favorite parking place and we fell out of the car, lugging our duffels. Fran had to take one handle of mine to help me carry it, I brought so much stuff. But no matter how much I brought, I always forgot something essential. There was a lot to bring: books and homework, clothes and towels and makeup, breakfast. Fran brought a hair dryer, too, but I liked going to class with wet hair. Fran must have been more secure than I was. I wanted people to know I was on the varsity swim team. The swimmers and the water-polo players

4

were the premiere athletes at Las Piedras High. Those were the only school teams that ever won anything.

We passed the pool on the way to the locker room; some of the boys on the water-polo team were already in the water. The deck lights were out but the underwater lights were on, so all you could see were these eerie shimmery bodies in the water. Suddenly there would be a big silvery splash as somebody else dived in. Because the deck was dark we couldn't see them coming and the splashes were a surprise. It was grand and mysterious there by the pool in the dark and I loved it. I felt like a member of a secret society.

We ran into the locker room and reluctantly peeled off our sweats to our suits underneath. Casey Meredith, the goalie on the water-polo team, told me some of the boys slept in their suits and sweats to speed things up for morning workouts. The cold speeded us up. Even in Southern California it is cold at 6:00 a.m. in October. We ran from the locker room and threw ourselves into the water to swim our five-hundred-meter warm-up.

"Everybody out of the pool!" Coach Halvorsen yelled, midway through the workout. "Sun up!"

We always had to get out of the pool to watch the sun come up. The coaches thought it was inspirational. Sometimes it was. There is such variety in sunrises. Some days the sun seems to pop up over the horizon—*boing!*—and it's morning. When it's foggy you can't really see the sun, just a bright core of light blurring off in the mist. Even the routine sunrises, which that Monday's was, are a miracle, it seems to me. I tried to write a science-fiction story once, about a time when the sun didn't come up, but I couldn't think of much except that it would always be dark and we wouldn't like going to the beach.

We all got out of the pool and wrapped up in our towels to "greet the dawn," as Coach Halvorsen called it. That was the first good look we got at the boys, since they were all trying to be tough and wouldn't huddle in their towels the way we did. They just stood there wet and shiny and shivering in those little suits that look obscene at the beach but are the only thing you can imagine a real swimmer wearing. Most of the reason we didn't mind morning workouts was that we got to swim with the water-polo team.

"Oh, my gosh," I said. "There he is."

"Kitty," Fran said, "when referring to Nicholas Arlington it is acceptable for you to say, 'Oh, my *God.*' "

"Oh, my God," I said. "I'm in love."

"I think you're in *lust,*" Fran said.

"It'll do."

Mary just stared. So did the rest of the girls' varsity.

There were a lot of good-looking boys on the water-polo team, and they all had terrific bodies, but there was something more than that to Nick; some kind of magnetism or charisma or x factor that made it hard to take your eyes off him. You could always tell when he was around because girls' heads turned in his direction, like daisies to the sun. Whatever he had, it made the other boys, no matter how good-looking they were, seem so juvenile.

Incredibly, Nick seemed unaware of his specialness. He'd arrived at Las Piedras High as an incoming senior the third day of school and, within about a week, seemed right at home.

A good deal of his easy transition was his outstanding athletic ability in water polo, the prestige sport at Las Piedras High. And part of it was his red Ferrari, I'm sure. But more than anything, he seemed to have an instinct for choosing the right people to associate with, and for conducting himself with just the correct blend of healthy self-confidence and respectful deference befitting a new boy in school.

That morning we stared at Nick, instead of at the sunrise, and then jumped back into the water, which seemed warm after we'd stood on the deck freezing, and finished our workout.

Something we all do while we swim is count laps and monitor our bodies to see if anything feels tight or hurts. After a while you can do that almost without thinking. Once, I asked some of the other girls what they thought about as they were swimming. A lot of them sang the Top Forty. Some reviewed homework or thought about their boyfriends or their wardrobes.

Families, that's what I thought about a lot. I guess because mine was so odd.

My parents got together in Haight-Ashbury in the sixties. My father says they were married when I was born, but I wonder. My father says my mother didn't do any drugs while she was expecting me, but I wonder about that, too. She didn't hang around long enough after I was born for me to ask her.

My father usually had a job, even though it often didn't last very long. Then, he was working in the produce department of a supermarket. But he considered himself an artist, not a produce person, and he wanted to live like an artist. That meant a loft with good north light and, a lot of the time, a live-in model.

As far as I could tell, he never considered himself a father, except in the biological sense. He had always, even when I was little, treated me like a roommate, with my own interests and activities that had nothing to do with his. He was pleasant enough to me, in an absent sort of way, but never seemed very concerned with what I was doing.

When I was six I fell while roller-skating, showing off for him as he came home from work, hoping, the way little kids do, that my roller-skating ability would prove to him what a valuable child I was. I split my lip badly enough to need stitches. I can still remember the way he looked around, as I lay on the sidewalk screaming and bleeding, for the person responsible for this troublesome little girl, before he remembered *he* was supposed to be the responsible party.

I haven't any grandparents or aunts or uncles or cousins that I know of. I'd never had a boyfriend. I'd never even had a pet. Doreen, the current live-in model, had a bird; that's the closest I've ever come to having a pet.

What I had were Mary and Fran. As far as I was concerned, they were my family, and they made up for everything else.

That morning I'm sure a lot of minds had discarded the Top Forty and homework and wardrobes as topics of concentration and were occupied with Nicholas Arlington fantasies. Mine was.

After workout came the scramble to get dressed, eat something, and get to class on time. I had remembered my underwear that day, but forgotten my hairbrush. I have a lot of curly hair, and when it's wet it's like mattress stuffing. I also hadn't tightened the cap on my thermos and Instant Breakfast was gluing together the pages of my history book. Mary loaned me her hairbrush while she went to shoot up. I struggled to drag the brush through my hair as I watched her take a hypodermic syringe and an ampule from her duffel, expertly suction the contents into the syringe, feel around on her thigh for a moment, and then inject herself. The first time I had seen her do that, it almost made me sick to my stomach, but by now I was so used to it I hardly noticed.

Then she sat down on the bench between the lockers and

8

drank orange juice from her thermos while she got dressed. She also ate a bagel, thickly spread with cream cheese, and a hard-boiled egg.

"Look at her *eat!*" I said to Fran, who was sharing the mirror with me. "I hardly eat anything and I can't lose an ounce, and she eats all the time and you can count her ribs."

"The only time you don't eat anything is at meals," Fran said. "Anyway, Mary has to be very careful about taking care of herself. She has to think about it all the time. You don't have the right kind of mind."

"Okay, okay," I said, popping my daily three almonds into my mouth. I had read somewhere that three almonds a day would prevent cancer. "Oh, my gosh, look at the time! I forgot to get out of the pool fifteen minutes early to do my Spanish! I've got to hustle!" I dug in my duffel for my clothes, spilling food, books, clothes, and makeup out around my feet.

Mary, who had probably never been late for anything in her life, buttoned up her dress, stuck her feet into her clogs, gave her hair one swipe with the brush, after which it looked perfect, and threw her brush into her duffel. Then she sat down to wait for Fran and me. Mary was always the first one ready, and she never looked as if she was hurrying.

Fran was ready next. All her clothes looked about the same —button-down shirts, Shetland sweaters, chino pants, and corduroy skirts—so getting dressed was practically an automatic process with her.

I was always last. I can't explain it. Fran said it was in my genes, from my rebellious parents, a disregard for society's conventions. I didn't see it that way at all, I would have loved a conventional life—I just seemed to be disorganized.

Finally we were ready and walked to class together. Most of the girls' varsity had raced through their dressing and rushed

9

outside to see if anybody could claim the privilege of walking to class with Nick Arlington. But he walked with his water-polo teammates. Because of that, every girl had hope. He hadn't indicated an interest in anybody since he started school. It could just as easily be me as anybody else. Improbable, maybe, but still possible.

Fran and Mary and I ate lunch together. Fran was indifferent to food. She always brought the same lunch: yogurt, an apple, and a banana. She said she didn't want to like anything that was seasonal because she'd have to think of something to replace it with when it was out of season. Mary brought huge healthy lunches packed by Mrs. Foster: tuna-salad sandwiches and thermoses of tomato soup, little cups of fruit salad and radish roses. Mrs. F. even tucked in one of those "moist towelettes" and a piece of dental floss in a plastic bag. She really took care of Mary.

A lot of the time I thought I needed to lose weight, so I'd bring a thermos of iced tea or chicken soup, but somehow I always ended up eating something from somebody else's lunch. Recently Doreen had been fixing me lunch. I didn't know if it was because she was trying to show my father what a good stepmother she'd make, though why anybody would want to marry my father was beyond me, or because she really liked me. She put in a lot of her vegetarian stuff, like sunflower seeds and dried apricots and peanut butter and honey balls, and often she included a little thought-provoking quote from something she'd read in the college English class she was taking. I liked Doreen.

That day I had avocado and sprouts on whole-wheat bread heavy enough to use as a doorstop. The quote for the day was "Happiness makes up in height for what it lacks in length— Robert Frost."

10

2

A couple of weeks later the three of us were sitting in the sun, eating and talking about how we were going to fall asleep in our after-lunch class, as we always did on morning workout days, when we looked up and there was Nicholas Arlington with an ice-cream bar in each hand. He swept us each with a smile and then settled it on Mary. He held the bar out to her and said, "Would you like some dessert?"

"I can't," Mary said. "But thank you, anyway."

"If you're worried about your figure, stop. It's perfect."

I swallowed so loud it made a funny noise in my throat.

"It's not that," Mary said. "It's not good for me."

"Once won't hurt," he said, still holding out the ice cream, although it was starting to melt and run down his fingers.

"Me it might," Mary said. "I'm diabetic."

Nick turned to Fran and me. "Ladies?" he said, holding the ice creams out to us. I didn't think twice. I took it. My fingers held the stick that, seconds before, Nick Arlington had held.

Fran didn't move, but Nick kept standing there, smiling at her and extending the ice cream until, finally, she took it.

Nick pulled a handkerchief from his pocket and wiped the drips from his hand as he turned back to Mary. "If I can't tempt you with ice cream, how about letting me walk you to your next class?" He held his hand out to her and she, looking hypnotized, took it. He pulled her up and they walked off, still holding hands.

Fran got up and threw her ice cream in the trash.

"Fran! What are you doing?" I asked. Mine was almost gone already.

"I hate those things," Fran said. "They taste so artificial and they melt too fast."

"But Nick Arlington gave it to you!"

She sat down next to me again. "It *still* tastes artificial and melts fast."

"No other girl would have done that."

She shrugged. "Fran's Law, proven again," she said. "I've never known it to fail. It usually applies to political and social issues, but this just shows you what a good law it is. It even applies to this small a situation."

"Which Fran's Law?" I asked. Fran has so many laws and rules and corollaries and imperatives I can't keep them all straight.

"He—or in this case, *she*— who needs the least gets the most," she informed me.

"What about what she deserves?"

Fran scowled, and her straight black bangs, which usually just touched the tops of her glasses, hung in her eyes. "Hardly anybody ever gets what they *really* deserve, good *or* bad. Hmmm. That would make a good corollary."

12

"Aren't you glad when somebody *does* get what they deserve, seeing as how it's so rare?"

"Sure. You think Mary deserves Nick?"

"Or somebody like him. She's got just about everything and so does he. They *should* be together."

"Have you considered the possibility of living a perfectly full and satisfying life without being *together,* of being individual?"

"Come on, Fran. Don't you think it would be more fun to be 'together'? Weren't you just the slightest little bit jealous when you saw Mary go off with that gorgeous hunk? Didn't you wish, for just a split second, that it was you instead of her?"

"You obviously did."

"What about you?"

She took a deep breath. "I think sex should be against the law. It causes more trouble than it's worth. Think of how productive people could be without all that distraction."

"Think how productive, literally, they are with it," I said.

"Look what a force the Catholic Church has been over the centuries," Fran said, as if she hadn't even heard me. When she got her teeth into an idea, you might as well sit down and listen. "And they're all celibate. Look what uncontrolled breeding has done to the world economically."

"We have to go to Biology," I said, standing up. "I'll mention your suggestion to Mrs. Stanley. Come on." She got up. "I hope I'm around to see what happens when the man for you comes along," I said.

"Ha!" she said. "It'll never happen. There's not a man out there strong enough to allow me my opinions and not be threatened by me."

"Never say never," I said. That was my only maxim; the only thought that really helped me. I liked to think that anything was possible, that any bad thing could change, that nothing was set in cement.

Still, one of the things I liked best about Fran was how definite she was, how sure. She had an opinion on almost everything you could think of and she could support her opinion. Look at all her rules. I, on the other hand, was so wishy-washy I couldn't make my mind up about anything. I could *always* see the other side, and it was terrible. Mary said I was the most tolerant person she knew, but it was really indecisiveness. My favorite phrase was "On the other hand . . ."

I was pretty sure about Nick Arlington, though. He was the most interesting boy I'd ever seen, and while Mary might have deserved him, I still wanted him.

In the car on the way home the only thing I wanted to hear about was Mary and Nick.

"What did he say, Mary? What did he talk about?" I asked.

"Not much," she said. "We only went as far as History together. He was interested in my diabetes."

"Are you going to see him again?"

"He's driving me to school tomorrow. I wouldn't have said yes if it had been my day to drive, but it's Fran's."

"I would have traded with you," Fran said.

"I know," Mary said. "But I wouldn't have wanted to. You're my best friends. I hardly know Nick."

"We'd have understood," I said. "Anyway, I think you're going to know him better."

"What makes you say that?"

"Mary, don't be so opaque," I said.

"Opaque?" Fran asked.

"You know, that new vocabulary word we had." We had been working on vocabulary building in English in preparation for S.A.T.'s.

14

"You mean obtuse," Fran said.

"Opaque, obtuse, what's the difference? Don't be so obtuse, Mary. You're the first girl here he's shown any interest in."

"Maybe he won't like me."

"Sure," I said.

"Maybe I won't like him."

"You jest," I said. "Stop being so sensible. If Nick Arlington had brought me an ice cream, I'd need CPR."

"He *did* bring you an ice cream," Mary said, laughing.

"No," I said. "He gave me *your* ice cream. That's different. Anyway, I know somebody like him would never be attracted to somebody like me. I'm too bland, too uninteresting. But you! You're beautiful and funny and unusual, and you have green eyes."

"Stop that! You are, too, interesting. Maybe he'll think *I'm* bland. Quit being so premature. Forget Nick. Let's go home and eat."

We often ended up at Mary's house after school. My loft wasn't conducive to our gatherings. You never knew who you'd find there. And Fran's house wasn't very welcoming. It was big and meticulously kept, full of heavy, dark, polished furniture, and her mother was so careful and worried about her possessions. I always felt as if my shirttail was out and I'd been caught wiping my nose on my sleeve when I was there. Fran's mother even wrote her name—Winifred—on each one of her clothespins.

Mrs. Foster was just right.

When we got there she was ironing sheets in the kitchen.

"Mrs. F.," Fran said, "there's these new things now called permanent-press sheets."

"I've heard of them," Mrs. Foster said, smiling at Fran, "but I love the feel of ironed percale sheets. That okay with you?"

"Help yourself," Fran said, sitting at the kitchen table. "I just thought most women wanted to be freed from the shackles of menial work in the service of others."

"Fran, dear," Mrs. Foster said, folding the sheet, "I know you have the best interests of women in mind, and that's admirable, but I hope someday you have somebody in your life you love enough to want to do things for."

"If he wants ironed sheets, he can iron them," Fran said.

Mrs. Foster laughed. "There's cookies in the cookie jar, and carrots and fruit in the fridge. Anything special you'd like, Kitty?"

"Don't worry, Mrs. F.," I said. "I'll help myself to everything, probably."

She put the iron on the drain board, collapsed the ironing board and put it away, and took her pile of ironed sheets upstairs. I wanted to move in.

We ricocheted around the kitchen fixing our favorite snacks, and finally settled at the table.

"You can come home with us after the meet tomorrow, Mary," Fran said. "Unless Nick comes to the meet and wants to bring you home."

"Why should he come to the meet?" Mary asked.

"To watch you swim, dummy," Fran said.

"Sounds improbable," Mary said, eating an apple slice.

We sat around the table, talking and gossiping, listening to our favorite radio station and giggling over nothing. Outside, the light changed as the afternoon passed.

"I've got to get home," Fran said. "My mother will be putting out an all-points bulletin."

"Me, too," I said, though there'd be no bulletin out for me.

"I'll take you," Mary said, getting up from the table and

looking for her car keys amid the heap of our duffel bags, sweaters, and purses.

When I got home Doreen was in the kitchenette slicing vegetables and throwing them into a pot. We always had lots of vegetables. My father brought home the ones too old to sell and used them as models for still lifes. Then we ate them. Being a vegetarian was practically an occupational hazard for him.

Doreen had on a leotard and a gauze skirt and sang as she sliced. She wore a lot of ethnic-looking clothes, which all looked about the same to me: gathered skirts in murky colors and tops with stripes or embroidery or patterns. I loved her jewelry, though. Long, beaded earrings and great clanking bracelets and big, important-looking necklaces. She had one from Africa, my favorite, that was hung with midwife tools. She was a lot younger than my father.

In the mornings she took her English class and modeled for art students at the college. In the afternoons she worked in a shop that specialized in monogrammed gifts. She got to bring home the ones that were ordered and never picked up. A lot of her possessions were monogrammed, but none of the initials were hers.

"Hi, Kitty," she sang. "Your dad's going to his How to Touch class tonight, so it's just us girls. How does minestrone sound to you?"

"Sounds good. Can I do anything?"

"No, no. This is fun. You just do your homework or your nails or whatever. I'll call you when it's done."

I walked the length of the loft, past the eating area, the living area, and the studio area to the only rooms with doors that closed: two bedrooms with a bath in between.

17

On the stained coffee table in the living room was a bowl of apples, and in the studio area a basket on a table before the easel spilled withered vegetables. Doreen did her best but the place still looked worn and motley, with none of the warm coziness of the Fosters' or the meticulous formality of Fran's.

In a while Doreen came and knocked on the door to my room to tell me dinner was ready. She had thrown a sheet, Sears budget polyester, over the little round table in the eating area and put a couple of candles and a bud vase, monogrammed *Nana*, holding three fresh carnations in the center of it. She lit the candles and turned off the lights. Two steaming bowls of soup and a basket of freshly baked bread awaited us.

"This is really pretty, Doreen," I said. "Turning out the lights improves this place no end."

She laughed. "If you grew up the way I did, this would look pretty good to you."

"How did you grow up?" I knew hardly anything about Doreen even though she had been living with us for a couple of months.

"Don't ask," she said. "It was awful. But I got myself out of there and I have plans for my future. This modeling and working at Brand Names is only temporary. Just to support myself until I finish school. Then I'm going to have a job where I put on a dress and stockings every day and look like somebody. And everything around me is going to be nice. I want to have something pretty to look at wherever I turn my head."

"What are you doing here, then?" I asked, sipping my soup.

"Your dad's an okay guy. You're a good kid. I like you both a lot. This is a good place for me to be right now."

"Sounds like you don't mean to stay." Maybe she *did* make my lunches just because she liked me. The thought pleased me.

"That's right. This is a place on the way, but it's not the

destination. Don't look like that, Kitty," Doreen said. "You didn't think I was here for keeps, did you?"

That was true, but I didn't want to think of her leaving. I liked having her around and I wanted things to stay the same for a while.

"I guess not."

"Your dad's a nice guy, but he's never going to be a grown-up, and I am. So are you."

Never say never, I hoped. "Me? Why do you say that?"

"Because I know. Kids with child-parents have to become grown-ups. But they do it the hard way, because they don't have anybody to show them how. While I'm here, you watch me. I'm still learning, too, but I'm ahead of you. I'll tell you the most important thing I've learned so far. Grown-ups take the consequences."

"The consequences?"

"For what they do. Always. Remember I said that. And grown-ups make plans. They don't just drift."

"Hmmm," I said, not sure what to say.

"The sooner you can start doing that, the better you'll be. Okay, Toots, I cooked the dinner. You can clean up. I've got to finish reading *Lord Jim* and figure out how to write a paper about it."

She stopped by her bird Onan's cage and whistled at him for a minute before she went into the bedroom to study. She said she'd named the bird Onan, after Dorothy Parker's bird, because he spilled his seed on the ground. She told me to look it up in the Bible, but I hadn't.

I took the dishes into the kitchen and turned on the hot water.

19

3

The next morning we went to school without Mary. I felt plain and dumpy chugging along in Fran's VW while Mary had graduated to a Ferrari.

At lunchtime Fran and I met in our usual place, but Mary never showed up.

Fran and I were on our way to Biology after lunch when Mary ran up to us in the hall.

"Where were you?" I asked.

"Off-campus lunch," she said. That was a privilege reserved for seniors, but Mary had never taken advantage of it before.

"With who?"

Her cheeks got pink. "Nick."

"I told you so," I said.

"My favorite words," she said. "Got to go. See you at the pool after school."

I drifted in to Biology and sat down. Immediately Casey Meredith sat next to me. "Hi, Kitty."

"Hi, Casey." I'd known Casey since fifth grade. Then we were Tom Sawyer and Becky Thatcher in the sixth-grade play. We worked on the school newspaper together in the seventh and eighth grades. We were both involved in student government in ninth grade, and we've swum together on school teams in tenth and eleventh grades. He'd always been part of my landscape, and had always been nice to me, as well as to everybody else, even when all the other boys were going through that unpleasant junior-high-school stage of pretending they hated girls and were playing all kinds of dumb pranks on me and my girlfriends.

"Who you swimming against today?" he asked.

"Bonita Valley. Tough guys."

"Yeah," he said. "Maybe I'll come watch you swim."

"Why?" I asked, surprised. The boys never came to watch us swim. They always had more important things to do. Of course, they expected us to come to their water-polo games. It was our duty and our privilege to be there to cheer them on. Fran refused to go to any games on principle. She had a law that said: Real men don't need groupies. Mary and I went occasionally, but Casey had never come to one of our swim meets.

"Fair's fair. You come to our games."

"Sometimes."

"Okay. So I'll go to yours sometimes."

"Great, wonderful," I said, still puzzled.

Mrs. Stanley came in and started class by handing back our last tests. "The fact that one of you believes the thyroid gland is located in the thigh indicates that you have not been paying the strictest attention in class," she said.

． ． ．

After school I walked over to the pool with Mary. In the
locker room we changed into our competition suits, which we
hated because they were practically transparent when wet.

"I think my blood sugar's going haywire," Mary said. She
had to constantly balance activity levels, food, insulin, and
emotional states to keep her blood sugar within normal limits.
She tested her blood sugar several times a day and then tried
to adjust the other facets of her life to keep it at the right level.
"I've been fiddling around with food and insulin, trying to get
things straight, but I feel weird."

"We'll keep an eye on you, then," I said. We watched out
for Mary. One of the biggest problems for a diabetic, even one
in such good control as Mary, is an insulin reaction. That
means too little sugar in the bloodstream as a result of too
much exercise or too much insulin or too little to eat or too
much emotional upset, or any combination. During an insulin
reaction Mary got weak and confused and irritable, or just
spacey. She also got terribly hungry. The cure was to give her
something sugary to bring up her blood sugar in a hurry. The
sugar could be in the form of candy or a soft drink or orange
juice. We always carried Life Savers or sugar cubes. Mary did,
too, but sometimes she was too confused to know what to do
with them when she was having an insulin reaction. She usually
got silly instead of mean like a lot of diabetics do. She tried to
put the Life Savers in her ears like earrings, and she giggled and
made up nonsense poetry. It took us a few times to figure out
what was going on, but we learned to recognize the signs, and
sometimes we knew a reaction was coming before Mary did.

Fran showed up then and started to change for the meet.

"Watch Mary," I told her. "She thinks her sugar's funny."

I pinned my good-luck charm, a first-place medal from the

first meet I ever swam in, to the inside of my suit and then put on a sweat shirt and went outside. I couldn't hold still, I never can before a meet. I shake my arms constantly to keep the muscles loose, and I hop around and talk a lot. I don't know how Fran does it. She sits on the bench, quiet, in her own little shell, storing up her energy. If I did that, I'd explode.

Mary, wearing her lucky Moosehead Beer cap, went around giving everybody little pep talks.

I was in such a state of nerves I almost ran into Casey before I noticed him.

"You *did* come," I said, bouncing up and down in front of him.

"I said I would. What's wrong with you?"

"Nerves. Once I swim my first event it's better. Pull my arms for me, okay?" There's nothing better than having your arms stretched before a race. It makes you feel as if you could make it across the pool in two strokes.

He took my hands and I leaned away from him. I was surprised at how gentle he was. He was so big, and when he played water polo, he was so aggressive, I half expected him to rip my arms right off. But he gave me such a mild tug I had to ask him to pull harder.

"I don't want to hurt you," he said.

"You didn't. Thanks. I've got to go swim now. Thanks for coming."

As I stood on the block waiting for the gun for the 200-meter individual medley, my favorite event, I saw Nick come through the gate to the pool. Then the gun sounded and the only thing I thought about was getting through the water as fast as I could.

I missed winning the race by eight-tenths of a second. I was so depleted I couldn't get out of the pool. I just hung on the

23

drain with my head down, trying to figure out how to move again. I felt hands on my arms and looked up to see Casey.

"Come on," he said. "They're ready for the next race."

He pulled me out, wrapped my towel around me, and sat me down on a bench. It took a few minutes for my nervous jangles to build up again.

While I sat on the bench with Casey, I watched Nick watching Mary. It was almost rude the way he stared at her. Any time I wanted to know where she was, I looked at his eyes and she was wherever they focused. I wanted to jump between her and him and yell, "Look at *me* that way, Nick! Me!"

Fran and Mary didn't like to be distracted during a meet. They stood together discussing times and stroke styles and the competition. Fran looked furious with concentration and Mary looked calm and grave.

Even at the break she didn't acknowledge Nick. I bounced and hopped and chattered and watched him.

Casey had to repeat himself twice before I heard. "You want to go to a movie Saturday night?"

"What?" I asked, dumbfounded when I realized what he'd said.

"You want to go to a movie Sat . . ."

"I heard right the first time, I guess," I interrupted. "Why, sure, I suppose that would be okay."

"Such enthusiasm. I want you to see this movie, *Inside Moves*. I've already seen it, but I want to see it again."

"Sounds good to me. I've got to go. I swim next." And I trotted off. What had come over old Casey? Typical. What I wanted was exciting Nick and what I got was my old fifth-grade pal Casey.

After I'd swum my last event, I pulled on my sweat shirt and

24

walked right up to Nick. I figured it was time he knew I was Mary's friend.

"Hi, Nick," I said. "It's nice of you to keep such a close eye on Mary. Almost like having a bodyguard."

"Ah, Kitty, my love," he said, surprising me by knowing my name and then by putting his arm around my shoulders. "It's a dirty job, but somebody has to do it."

I laughed and felt as if I had been touched with a magic wand. I was standing there and Nick Arlington had his arm around me! In front of everybody! And just because I was a friend of Mary's. What if I were Mary? I would probably be in insulin shock.

The gun went off then for Mary's last event, the 500-meter freestyle, and we both turned to watch her. She was beautiful in the water, swimming with the smoothest, most efficient stroke you ever saw.

The 500 free is the longest race, twenty lengths of the pool, and it is hard. You have to have plenty of endurance and be able to pace yourself. This is the kind of event you either love or hate. Nobody is indifferent to 500 meters.

Mary won, of course. She usually did. When she hit the wall she collapsed in the shallow water with her head down on the gutter, the way swimmers usually do at the end of a hard race.

But Mary stayed there so long I started to get worried, especially when I remembered what she had said before the meet about her sugar being upset. I looked over to where Fran was waiting and saw her watching Mary, too. Mary still hadn't moved.

"Something's wrong with Mary," I said, and reluctantly moved away from Nick. Fran was heading for the side of the pool then, too, as well as the official, who was interested in clearing it for the start of the next event.

25

I reached down into the water and took her forearms. "Mary," I said. "Mary, are you all right."

She lifted her head as if it weighed a metric ton and gave us this loopy grin. "Actually," she said, "I think I'm all left. Or maybe even all port or all starboard. Perhaps all fore or all aft. All leeward or . . ."

Fran looked at me, rolled her eyes, and grabbed Mary's arms, too. We heaved and dragged her out of the pool, wrapped her in a towel, and led her over to a concrete bench where my duffel bag was. I rummaged around until I found a little plastic bottle full of sugar cubes and shook out three of them. It was times like that I was glad I always carried so much stuff in my duffel.

"Open wide," I said to Mary. "Here's one for Mommy and here's one for Daddy and here's one for Grandma. Now eat them up like a good girl."

Mary downed the sugar cubes and then just sat there grinning goofily and waiting for her blood sugar to rise, which took about fifteen minutes. We had been through this before with her and knew there was nothing to get agitated about. Coach Halvorsen came over to see what was going on and was satisfied when I told her we'd taken care of it.

While I was sitting with Mary waiting for her to shape up, I happened to look over at Nick, who was still standing where I had left him. I don't know if I can describe his face, since I had never seen an expression like that before. The best I can do is to say it was a combination of fear and fascination. I got up and walked over to him again.

"It's okay, Nick," I said. "It's just an insulin reaction. She'll be okay as soon as her blood sugar gets back up. It's nothing to worry about. Really."

26

"Does she do this very often?" he asked, still looking at her as if he had never seen her before.

"Not too often, but you have to know what to do when it does happen or it can be serious. It's simple. She just needs to have a couple of sugar cubes. It happens to all diabetics, even ones like Mary who are very careful about everything. Sometimes it seems to happen for no reason that you can figure out. But really, it's okay."

He seemed to relax a little bit. "Come on over and talk to her. She's through swimming now and you won't upset her concentration."

"You sure?" He still looked panicked. I remembered the first time I had seen Mary have an insulin reaction, but I didn't remember feeling the way Nick looked. But maybe I had at first. When I found out what to do about it and how fast she got better, I quit worrying, but I guessed everybody was different, and especially if Nick really liked Mary, I could see how he would be worried about something happening to her.

I led him over to her. By that time she was almost herself again, and when she talked to him she made sense. His face relaxed and he sat down next to her, unselfconsciously took her hand, and said, "I was worried about you."

I could see she was in good hands, literally, so I went into the locker room to get dressed. I figured Mary'd be along when she was good and ready, and since we weren't giving her a ride home, it didn't matter anyhow.

Fran was standing at the mirror in her underwear, combing out her hair. She trimmed her bangs every Saturday morning to keep them just long enough to touch the top of her glasses. When she swam she took off her glasses, of course, and with her wet bangs slicked back, she looked so unfamiliar as to be frightening. It was always a relief to see Fran back again, transformed from the thin, bangless, glasses-less arrow of concentration that she was during swim meets.

"Mary okay?" she asked.

"More than merely okay," I said, "Nicholas Arlington is sitting with her holding her hand."

"I think this is going to develop into something."

"Just what we all dream about," I said wistfully.

"Speak for yourself. That's not a very liberated viewpoint,"

"I know, I know. My consciousness is as raised as anybody's but, I don't know, maybe biology is destiny. I still think it would be wonderful to fall in love and live happily ever after."

"Huh!" she snorted. "At least promise me you won't do that until you have your MBA from the Harvard Business School, own your own car, and have a Swiss bank account full of your separate property."

"Sure, sure."

Mary came floating into the dressing room then, looking just as goofy as she had when we pulled her out of the pool, but for a different reason. I snapped my fingers in front of her face. "Earth to Mary, Earth to Mary, come in please."

She giggled.

"I'm giving you a subscription to *Ms.* for Christmas," Fran said.

Mary passed blissfully by us to the showers. Through the roar of the water we heard her yell, "Do either of you have a date Saturday night?"

"May I inquire why you want to know before committing myself?" Fran asked.

"Because I'm looking for somebody to double-date with," Mary yelled back. The noise of the water stopped and in a minute she came out of the shower, her towel tucked around her, trailing puddles.

28

"I wonder if I can guess who you're going out with," Fran said.

"I bet you could if you tried *real* hard," Mary said.

"*I* have a date," I said. "With Casey."

Fran and Mary both turned and looked at me. "Casey?" they asked.

I shrugged. "He asked me. I said okay. That's it. Why do you want to double?" I asked Mary.

"Security, I guess," she said. "That way, if Nick and I are awkward together, we'll have somebody else to talk to."

"I got the distinct impression you were anything but awkward together," Fran said.

"But we've never been on a date. That might be different. Come on, Kitty, will you go with us?"

"I guess so, if it's okay with Nick. The only thing is, Casey really wants to see this movie, *Inside Moves*. Do you think Nick would want to see that?"

"If I ask him," Mary said confidently.

4

Mary and Nick were instantly a couple. Before they had even had their first official date, everybody knew they went together. The morning after the swim meet, word had already spread about how attentive Nick had been to Mary after she had her insulin reaction. They arrived at school together in his red Ferrari. They were together at lunchtime and between classes. By the end of the week it was as if they had always gone together. There was an inevitable logic about it. They were both bright, beautiful, special; designed for each other. I felt dull and plain by comparison, and clearly outclassed.

While Nick was friendly with everybody, he went out of his way to be nice to Fran and me. Friday morning he took the three of us to school, piled in his car with the top down, and I enjoyed the stir we caused when we arrived in the parking lot, windblown and laughing. I liked basking in the reflected glow of the dazzle generated by Mary and Nick.

They were pure glamour, something I would never be and was therefore drawn to. Maybe it was frivolous, but I liked being associated with them, borrowing some of their shine, since I had none of my own. I wondered, as always trying to see both sides of the question, if any glamorous person would wish she could switch places with me and get out of the spotlight for a while. It seemed unlikely.

Fran was above my kind of yearning. She liked being with Mary because she liked Mary. She accepted Nick since he was accompanied by Mary. To be accepted on his own merits, he would have to prove himself to her, something he hadn't done yet.

"Don't be such a pushover for a pretty face," she said to me.

"Don't forget the pretty car," I said.

"Or for a pretty car. Look behind the mask."

"What makes you think it's a mask?"

"Everybody wears a mask, at least some of the time. That's one of my laws."

"Oh. Well, if that's true, I wish my mask was as good as his."

"You wear a mask less than anybody I know, and *need* one less, too."

"Why, Fran!" I said. "Well, thank you."

"You're welcome," she said.

At lunch that Friday, Nick brought Mary a button that said "Angelface" and pinned it to her sweater. She was embarrassed, but flattered, too, as what girl in her right mind wouldn't be, and finally agreed to leave it on. Everybody knew where she had gotten it and the girls were awed by such a romantic gesture. I don't know how the boys felt, but I hoped it gave them ideas. That same day I had a note from Doreen in my lunch sack that said, "He that riseth late must trot all day—Benjamin Franklin." The comparison between Mary's gift and mine did not bear contemplation.

I began to wonder if I wanted to double-date with them on Saturday. It seemed a sure bet they weren't going to have any trouble relating, and I wasn't certain I was up to the strain of watching all that perfection without wanting to go home and put my head in the oven. Since we have an electric oven, I guess nothing would happen even if I did, unless I left it in there long enough to bake it.

There was a water-polo game after school on Friday, and since Nick had brought us to school, he was also our ride home, so we had to stay for the game. Fran grumbled endlessly about that and threatened to wait in the car with a book.

But we dragged her with us, and we found seats on the poolside benches. Fran immediately buried her nose in her biology book while Mary and I watched the boys get ready. If they had the same kind of nervousness as the girls did before a meet, it didn't show. They joked and pushed each other around until it was time to jump in the pool.

Once in the pool, both teams lined up along the side and put their hands up on the edge to be inspected by the referee.

"You there, on the Green team," the referee said, "too long." The boy with the offending hands scrubbed his nails back and forth on the concrete of the deck, ostensibly filing them but probably just making them ragged enough to do more damage.

Water polo is a rough game as well as a strenuous one. A lot goes on under water that the officials never see. Even though all the players must have their fingernails checked before the game starts, there is still a lot of underwater scratching. Also kicking, punching, and poking. Having a suit torn off is not unusual either; a lot of the guys wear two suits for that very

32

reason. When one is torn, they just let it drop to the bottom of the pool and keep playing in the second suit. I don't know what they do when the second suit gets torn, but I keep hoping I'll be at a game when that happens.

It was always hard for me to figure out what was going on in water polo. There was so much yelling and splashing and whistle-blowing for such a basically simple game. Since I went to games more to watch the players than the play, though, it didn't matter if I really understood the fine points. I usually noticed who made the goals and who made the fouls, and in the great cosmic scheme of things, what else matters?

I did like to watch Casey. He was a great goalie. Partly because he was so big. He just plain filled up a lot of the goal space. He was also fast, surprisingly, for someone his size. He had an uncanny ability to figure out which way to jump at the same instant the ball was thrown. He almost always got to the place the ball was going before the ball did.

But at that game I watched Nick. Not only because of Mary, who was focused on him the same way he had been on her at our meet, but because he was so good. He was left-handed, a decided advantage in water polo. He could catch and throw with the hand closest to the action without having to reach across his body as a right-handed player has to do. He also swam a strong backstroke, another good thing to do well, since a player is often swimming down to the goal at the same time as he is waiting for the ball to be thrown to him.

The ball flew back and forth, there was plenty of shouting —some of which I understood and some of which I didn't, and it was probably a good thing, too—a lot of splashing, a lot of fouls, and we scored a couple of goals.

In the second quarter the number of Nick's fouls increased and he had to stay out more. A player can be ejected from the game for only thirty seconds for each personal foul, but Nick's time-outs were adding up to several minutes.

The coach was watching Nick, too. At poolside between the third and fourth quarters, I heard him say, "Watch the roughness, Arlington." And that seemed to do it. Nick played outstanding polo, and in the fourth quarter he made two goals and assisted in another. He looked like an ideal player—talented, fast, aggressive, and obedient. The same kind of athlete as Mary. A perfect match.

5

I was ready long before Casey arrived Saturday night. I couldn't envision him sitting on the rump-sprung sofa in the living room watching my father paint Doreen in the almost-nude while I finished dressing.

"Dad, *please,*" I'd begged. "Can't you wait until I'm gone to paint Doreen?"

"How about it, Stan?" Even Doreen was on my side. "Give the kid a break."

"I push turnips around the whole week," my father said, "and I must maximize my time to paint. Apparently you don't understand my needs and the level of my artistic frustration. Any boy who would be upset by watching an artist at work isn't worthy of you, anyway, Kitty."

"Okay, okay," I muttered. I saw his point, but he never seemed able to see mine. I was sure it wouldn't upset Casey to watch an artist at work. I just didn't want the artist to be my father, painting an undressed woman who lived with us.

Doreen arranged herself in a chair and allowed a black chiffon scarf to settle haphazardly over her.

Casey knocked on the door and I opened it just enough to be able to squeeze through.

"Kitty," my father called when I'd almost made it, "I'd like to meet your friend."

"We're in a hurry, Dad," I said through gritted teeth. If I hadn't made an issue of Doreen, he wouldn't have insisted on meeting Casey. I couldn't decide if what I felt was sadness or anger when he acted like that—more of a child than I was, less of an adult. When would I learn? When would I stop expecting him to act like something he wasn't?

"It's okay," Casey said. "We have time."

Reluctantly I opened the door. "Dad and Doreen, this is Casey Meredith"; then I turned and pushed Casey back out the door he had just come through. "Good night," I called back to them, and closed the door.

Casey and I clattered down the two flights of wooden stairs. "So your dad's still painting?" Casey asked.

"A little," I said. "He works in a supermarket, too."

"I didn't know he'd gotten married again."

"They're not married."

"Oh."

We got in Casey's car. He didn't start the engine. "Kitty," he said, turning to face me, "I don't care who Doreen is or what your dad does. I don't want to take *them* to the movies."

It was my turn to say "Oh." Casey started the car.

We met Nick and Mary at the Fosters', and we went to the

movie together in Casey's car. Nick wanted to take his, but Casey was too big to fit into the back seat.

"I never heard of this movie, Casey," Nick said. "What's it about?"

"Basketball. And handicaps. Body and mind handicaps. There's a guy with a bad leg who's always wanted to play basketball, but he can't because of his leg. He works in a bar where all these handicapped people hang out. There's a blind guy and a crippled guy and a guy with hooks instead of hands. They all take care of one another. Then the guy with the bad leg has an operation and it fixes his leg, and he gets to play basketball on a good team. He forgets about the people in the bar. Then something happens that makes him remember what special friends they were to him. It's a good movie."

It *was* a good movie. All about courage and love and triumph over adversity. I could have seen it a couple of times myself.

Nick and Mary held hands, and Casey and I ate. Casey ate as if it were an Olympic event. Even though he had already seen the movie, he was reluctant to go for food in the middle and miss something, so he stocked up before we went in: popcorn, Cokes, Junior Mints, Ju Ju Bits, Reese's Pieces, and long red ropes of licorice. It was awe-inspiring to watch him eat. And with his hands full of food, I didn't have to worry about him trying to hold mine.

After the movie he was hungry, so we went across the street to Señor Wong's for a hamburger. In big red letters over the front door it said IT'S ALWAYS WIGHT TO EAT AT WONG'S.

Casey had his hamburger and the rest of us had Chinese tea and tortilla chips, and we talked about the movie.

"Wasn't that a neat movie?" I asked.

"I loved it," Mary said.

"Mumph," Casey said, around his hamburger.

"I didn't like it," Nick said.

"*What?*" the rest of us said together. "Why not?"

"I don't know. It made me uncomfortable, all those crip-ples."

"But that's the point of the movie," Casey said. "That underneath, they're like anybody else."

"I don't think they are," Nick said. "How could they be? Their whole lives are so different."

"Yeah," Casey said, "but the important stuff—love, loyalty, having fun—that's the same."

Nick shook his head. "Being handicapped like that, it has to change you somehow."

"Maybe it can make you better," Mary said. "Beethoven was deaf. Homer was blind. Helen Keller was deaf *and* blind. President Roosevelt was crippled." She paused. "Cézanne and Ernest Hemingway and Thomas Edison were diabetics."

Nick stubbornly shook his head. "Exceptions."

Mary shrugged. "Still . . ."

"Anyway," I said, "it was a good movie." I didn't want to hear any more of what Nick was saying. How could he talk that way in front of Mary?

"I'm glad you liked it," Casey said. "I thought you would."

Then he and Nick started talking about water polo, and Mary and I looked at each other and rolled our eyes and began our own conversation. After quite a few minutes of being ignored, Mary turned to Nick and said, "Nick, your hair is on fire."

He stopped talking to Casey and turned to look at her.

"I wondered if you were paying attention," she said.

He laughed and laced his fingers through hers, and she looked at him as if she had just won a prize.

38

"Sorry," he said. "That was rude of me. I didn't mean to neglect you."

We took them back to the Fosters' and then Casey drove me home.

"I didn't like the way Nick was talking," Casey said. "Especially in front of Mary."

"Me neither. But I don't think he meant to hurt her."

"I guess not. It's easy to forget Mary's diabetic."

"I know. It's just part of her, like green eyes or curly hair. I know it's hard for her, but she never makes it seem like a handicap."

"That's why I liked that movie. Those guys were trying to live as if they weren't handicapped, too."

"I've never known anybody with a *real* handicap. I mean, like being blind or having no legs. I can't imagine what that would be like."

"Neither can I," Casey said. "I had a dog once with a twisted leg. He was born that way and the owners were going to put him to sleep because they couldn't sell him. But I took him instead and he turned out to be a great dog. He slept on my bed every night and he learned all kinds of tricks. He was smarter and more affectionate than any dog I ever knew."

"What happened to him?"

"He got hit by a car when I was thirteen. He saw the car coming, but because of his leg he couldn't get out of the way fast enough and it hit him. The guy never even stopped, either. I was standing on the front porch and I saw it happen. I started running even before the car hit him, but I couldn't get there in time." He hit the steering wheel with his fist.

"How awful!" I almost put my hand over Casey's fist, but

39

I decided not to. "I've never had a pet. Maybe it's a good thing."

"I'm not sorry I had him. He was worth it."

When I got home I said, "It's okay, Casey, you don't have to walk me upstairs."

"I'm responsible for you until you're in the door. Anybody could be lurking on the stairs. This isn't the best neighborhood, you know."

"Wait a minute. *You're* responsible for *me?* Don't you read the paper? Don't you listen to Fran? That's out of date. Everybody's responsible for themselves these days. Men no longer have to take care of women. Women are capable of taking care of themselves."

"Maybe so. Maybe I'm an old-fashioned male chauvinist pig. I can't help it. I'm bigger and stronger than you are and I asked you out tonight and that makes me responsible for your safety. It must be atavistic, but I look after the people I care about."

"Atavistic, huh? We had that one this week, too."

He grinned. "A word's not yours until you use it," he said, quoting Mr. Roxburgh, our English teacher. He drummed his fingers on the back of the car seat, then abruptly turned and opened the door. I sat. He came around and opened my door. He took me by the elbow and guided me up the wooden stairs to the top floor.

We stopped in the dim hallway in front of my door. He still held me by the elbow, so I couldn't get into my purse for my key.

"Thanks, Casey. It was fun. I liked your movie."

He just stood there holding my arm and looking at me. "I

meant it," he said. "I want to look after the people I care about."

"I believe you," I said, puzzled.

"I care about you, Kitty."

Oh oh. "I care about you, too, Casey. We've been friends for a long time," I said nervously.

He took my other arm in his other hand and stood, facing me, holding my arms. I was suddenly freshly aware of how big and strong he was.

"What is it, Casey? You're scaring me."

Solemnly he leaned forward and kissed me. I wasn't much of an expert on kissing, but I couldn't imagine how a kiss could be much better than the one I got from Casey. Some things happened to my breathing and my heart rate and my knees that I hadn't experienced before. Somehow my arms went up around Casey's neck and his went around me, and some more kisses, even better than the first one, ensued.

What's going on here, I thought. Casey's my old buddy, my pal, my classmate. *Nick's* the one I'd like to be doing this with. Then how come my old buddy is making me feel as if I've been hit by a bus while running a fever?

"Casey, Casey, wait a minute, stop," I murmured against his cheek. "This is too confusing." I put my hands on his chest and pushed, trying to put some daylight between us, but it was like pushing a building. "Please."

He loosened his grip on me. "Did I offend you?" he asked earnestly.

I laughed shakily. "Surprised me is more like it. I wasn't expecting anything like that."

"I'm sorry. I couldn't help it."

"I've just never thought of you like . . . well, like that. I mean, we're *friends.*"

41

"I hope so."

"I better go in, Casey. I need to think about, um, things."

"Okay," he said, folding me against him and hugging me gently. "I'll call you."

"Fine," I said, digging in my bag for my key. He took it from me, turned it in the lock, and pushed the door open.

Doreen had left a thick white candle, printed with HAPPY BIRTHDAY, ANGELA, burning on the coffee table, a romantic but stupid thing to do with all the paint and turpentine around. Its glow softened the long room and made it look charming and interesting. Odd how different things can look when viewed in another light.

I gave Casey a little shove and closed the door. "Good night." I hadn't really needed to shove him. My hand just wanted to touch him again.

I blew out the candle and went to the big windows running the length of the room. The street lamp outside cast enough light so that the candle had been unnecessary. I stood and watched Casey, three stories below, get into his car and drive away.

I went into the bathroom and looked at myself in the mirror. I couldn't believe my outside looked so calm when my inside was so agitated. It didn't seem to matter what went on inside my head: my body had a will of its own that I didn't understand at all.

What a strange evening. That emotional movie. And the way Nick talked about handicaps in front of Mary. The way Mary looked at him when he took her hand. The way he looked at her. And Casey! Then there was the way I responded to Casey. I shook my head at my reflection, and she gave me a quizzical smile.

I washed my face, pulled on the men's XXXL T-shirt I wore to bed, and escaped into sleep.

．　．　．

Casey did call me Sunday evening when I'd gotten home from the Petrified Florist, the artificial-flower shop where I worked weekends and two days a week after school.

We didn't talk about anything important, and neither of us referred to Saturday night. I liked the way he sounded on the phone—big and safe and calm. Not exciting, though. Not like Nick. Not glamorous. Just nice.

After I talked to Casey I made some popcorn and started my normal Sunday night round of calls, an essential part of postponing homework. First, I called Mary.

"Can I call you back later?" she asked. "Nick's here. We're doing homework." Then she laughed, a happy excited laugh with a little throb of something else in it, and I had a feeling they weren't doing much homework. A stab of envy hit me and it hurt.

Then I called Fran. "Can you talk?"

"Sure. I've been studying but I need a break. How was the double date? Did Mary and Nick have a good time?"

"Mary and Nick had a good time—are still having it from the sound of things. He's at her house now. I'm trying to figure out how to clone him for my biology project."

She laughed. "That would make you very popular with a lot of girls. How's old Casey?"

"Old Casey is . . . interesting."

"What does that mean?"

"He seems bigger than he used to be."

"What?"

"Never mind." I wasn't ready to talk about him yet. I obviously didn't know what to say.

"What are you eating now?" she asked me.

"Just popcorn. It's low-cal."

"If you'd lose ten pounds it'd take seconds off your two hundred IM time."

"Nag, nag, nag. I like being rounded."

"Why?" Fran was lean and tense and, as usual, could only see things her way.

"I'm cuddly."

"You mean you're maintaining your body for somebody else to cuddle?"

Oh, Lord. "Well, not exactly."

"Kitty, you need to think these things through. If you like being plump"—I cringed—"because it makes you cuddly, does that mean you like to cuddle yourself?"

"Can we change the subject?"

Fran laughed. "Sorry. I've been preparing for Debate Club and it makes me contentious."

"Insufferable."

"Persistent."

"Obnoxious."

"Tenacious."

"Offensive. Odious. Abominable. Halcyon."

"Halcyon? You better look that one up again. Okay, I get the message. What do *you* want to talk about?"

"Love." I couldn't help myself. It was on my mind. "I'm so scared I'll never be in love, that there'll never be anybody like Nick for me, that I'll go through life attracting people I'm not interested in, or card-carrying goons."

"Love! Spare me! A momentary physiological attraction for one purpose only—the continuation of the species. Consider divorce rates. Child abuse. Wife beating. Desertion. Romeo and Juliet were two histrionic adolescents overwhelmed by their hormones. Tristan and Isolde, Héloïse and Abélard, Antony and Cleopatra, Daphnis and Chloë, they all came to bad ends. Hardly a recommendation for love."

44

"Do you think so? I thought love made the world go round. That it redeems the worst brute. It's the basis of almost every religion, in some form or other. Do you really think it's just hormones?" I became indecisive as usual. "Maybe we do mistake animal needs and urges for something more romantic. Maybe we just dress it up as love to fool ourselves. Or to console ourselves." The thought made me feel desolate.

"I believe in some kinds of love absolutely," Fran said. "The more abstract the better: love of country, devotion to principle, charitable love. As for romantic love, well, I guess I believe in the *possibility* of that kind of love. I just don't think it actually happens very often. I don't know why people think they have to fall into it. Business deals, which marriages are, should never be made on such an insubstantial basis."

I sighed. Was my attraction to Nick purely hormonal? Was Mary's? What about Casey? How did Fran avoid getting mixed up in such snarls?

"But I know there is such a thing as love," Fran continued. "I love you and Mary. I'd do anything for you. That's what love is, I guess. When it works."

"Oh, Fran," I said, tears pricking my eyes. "You know I feel that way, too. I'd be sunk without the two of you. You're my sisters."

Fran cleared her throat. "Anyway, there's six and a half million more women than men in the world, you know."

"What wonderful news."

"I thought you'd be glad to hear that. Now I have to go finish my homework. You do, too."

"Right. I'll see you in the morning."

45

6

The next morning after workout, while we were dressing in the locker room, a girl on the team lit a joint and passed it around. None of the three of us ever indulged, but for different reasons. Mary because it wasn't good for her diabetes; Fran because she was contemptuous of what she called crutches; me because, for one thing, I'd never gotten up the nerve, and for another, I'd never decided whether I should or not.

Las Piedras means the rocks or the stones in Spanish. Sometimes I thought it should mean the stoned. There were lots of kids smoking dope at school. I didn't even like to go to the bathroom there because of the aroma that lingered from between-class joints.

Monday at lunch I was complaining about it to Fran. "Honestly, I get high just walking past the bathroom. And that stuff stinks!"

"I wonder what it would feel like to get really high," Fran

said. "It must be good or so many people wouldn't be doing it."

"Don't you worry about what it might do to your body?" I asked. My father smoked a lot of pot, and sometimes I wondered if it had anything to do with his inability to grow up. "I already overindulge in enough other things that affect my body, like chocolate. At least it doesn't do anything to my chromosomes or my brain cells. *You* already OD on opinions and politics."

Fran just raised an eyebrow and turned back to her yogurt and we talked about something else.

After lunch, in Biology, Casey sat down next to me and I said, "Casey, have you ever done any drugs?"

He looked surprised. "Why do you ask?"

"Curiosity. I just wondered if any of the so-called normal people I know had."

"Well, sure, I've smoked some. Not for a long time, though. I guess I was curious, too."

"What was it like?"

"It felt good, mellow. I liked it, all right. But it was expensive and I didn't have the right mentality for it. I was always afraid of getting busted. Also, it made me too serious and somehow it made me feel lonely. So, I'll just have to be mellow on my own, with no chemical help."

"Oh, Casey," I said, overwhelmed.

"You thinking of becoming a stoner?"

"No. Just living vicariously."

"Vicariously."

"Use it once and it's yours."

He grinned and put his big hand on mine for a moment before the bell rang.

47

・　・　・

In the car on the way home I said, "Fran, remember what you were talking about at lunch?"

"What? Getting high?"

"Yeah."

"What about it?"

"My father smokes. He just sits in a chair and stares. He says it improves his inner vision for painting."

"Hmmm," she said. "Supposedly Coleridge wrote 'Kubla Khan' in an opium stupor but he got interrupted and then couldn't remember how he meant to end the poem, so he never finished it."

"Most of my father's pictures look like he couldn't remember how to finish them either."

Fran laughed. "Do you know where he keeps his stuff?"

"Sure. Why?"

"Just curious. Aren't you?"

"Are you suggesting what I think you're suggesting?"

Mary was quiet the whole time and I thought she was concentrating on driving. Suddenly she said, "Why not? Everybody else does it. Once won't kill us. Think of it as an experiment."

I gaped. This was coming from Mary? Mary who always made her own decisions independent of what "everybody else" did? Mary who had to worry about her body more than the rest of us did? Mary who'd always had an almost puritanical code of behavior?

"What?" I said.

"I'm graduating in June," Mary said. "And I'll be going to college, a complete innocent. It's dangerous. I need some experience before I leave home. What better way to get it than with you guys. We can look out for each other and we don't have

48

to worry about making fools of ourselves and we can be discreet."

"Wow," Fran said. "What an idea!"

I looked at Fran and Mary and felt as if I was going to cry. "Are you sure this is a good idea? What if something happens? What if we overdose? What if we get caught? What if we *like* it?"

"Now, Kitty," Fran said, "don't be such an alarmist. Think of it as an experiment in human biology. Merely one minor experience in life's colorful panoply."

"Panoply?"

"You get the idea. Come on, don't spoil it. Think how little time the three of us have left to spend together. This time next year, Mary'll be in college."

"Well, okay," I said reluctantly. "You should have a responsible person along, I suppose, in case anything does go wrong."

"You're the responsible person?" Fran asked, her eyebrows raised.

"Fran," Mary said soothingly, "Kitty's very responsible."

"Sure, sure she is," Fran said. "Okay, it's settled. Now, where? When?"

"My father and Doreen are going camping this weekend," I said. "With one of those groups my father belongs to. You can come to my place."

"Make sure you get some, um, supplies before he goes," Fran said. "What if he takes it with him?"

"Okay," I said.

"While we're at it . . ." Fran said.

"What now?" I asked apprehensively.

"Well, why not try some other things, too? Booze, cigarettes, wild . . ."

"Fran!" I said. "Have you gone crazy?"

She laughed. "I'll bring the whip and the leather and we can get kinky!"

I stared at her, speechless.

"Fran's just joking," Mary said, patting my knee. "Don't worry, Kitty. Don't you know us better than that?"

"I thought so," I said. "But you're both acting so weird. It's scaring me."

"Be reasonable," Fran said. "Mary has a point. It's dangerous to be as innocent as we are. If we know how we act under the influence, we won't discover in public someday that one glass of wine makes us take our clothes off. Think of it as insurance." She paused. "I'll bring the booze. My dad'll never miss it."

"Do you really want to smoke cigarettes?" Mary asked. "Other than the mind-altering kind, of course. Somehow that habit has never had the slightest attraction for me. I can't imagine being tempted by one."

"Me neither," I said. "You can try it if you want, Fran, as long as you're trying every other vice and perversion."

"I guess you're right, Mary," Fran said. "Okay, booze and dope ought to be good enough for one night. Unless you'd like to provide some hard drugs, Kitty. Or a few chocolate cakes?"

"That's not funny," I sniffed.

My father and Doreen left Friday afternoon on their camping trip. All day Saturday at the Petrified Florist I was jumpy and preoccupied. On the one hand, I was excited. On the other, I was scared to death something would go wrong—one of us would overreact to something and go into a coma, the cops would raid us, drinking *would* make me want to take off my clothes—and that my caution and reluctance were perfectly justified.

50

Mr. Andrade had to speak to me so many times about my inattentiveness he finally said, "Go home! I'll close up. Today you aren't even worth the pittance I pay you. Scram!" So I went home.

Usually I like it when nobody but me is there for a meal. Sometimes I like to be able to get sensuous with my food in a way you can't do in public. I recognize the social value of eating in groups, but not every time. There are certain comfort foods I like to more or less wallow in. Like bananas and oatmeal and pudding. I like to swish them mushily back and forth in my mouth like mouthwash and enjoy that soft, full feeling. I could hardly do that at the dinner table. Also, I like food combined with other food in casseroles, or what my father calls "your disgusting messes." Just because he won't eat rice, cheese, refried beans, and mushrooms melted together doesn't mean it's disgusting.

I was looking forward to making one of my messes, but when I got home my stomach was upset and I was disappointed to find I didn't want to eat. Just before Fran arrived I was able to drink a glass of milk. I figured it would be smart to lay down a base of something before the festivities began.

Fran came breezing in, lugging her duffel bag. "Boy, if my father only knew what I have in here! My parents dropped me off on their way to a party and I wanted to say, 'Tonight I taste *life!* Next time you see me I'll no longer be your little girl but a *woman!*"

"Don't you think that's going a bit far?"

"Maybe," Fran said, eyeing the portrait of Doreen on my father's easel.

I threw a cover over the canvas. I'd tidied up as much as I could, but I wished it would get dark. Low lights improved the place no end. "I'll be back in a minute," I said to Fran. I went into the bathroom and took out my contacts. I don't feel quite like myself when I can't see clearly and I thought a little distance from the forthcoming events might be a good idea.

When I came back, Mary had arrived. She was pink-cheeked and excited-looking, and I wondered if it was her blood sugar or if she was simply as eager as Fran was to get on with this evening of dissipation.

Fran and Mary gleefully began to unpack the bottles of booze from Fran's bag and line them up on the coffee table. Fran went to the kitchen for glasses. Then she brought my stereo from the bedroom and turned it to our favorite station. Loud and thumping music filled the loft. I felt like a nun at an orgy.

"Does anybody want something to eat?" I asked nervously.

Nobody did. After some discussion, while I sat on the lumpy couch with my arms folded across my chest, we decided to smoke first. We wanted to experience each vice as purely as possible, but we were so ignorant we didn't know which took effect fastest or which wore off quickest. So we made an arbitrary choice. Also, I, like Casey, worried about getting caught and I wanted to get the most dangerous part over with first.

I had taken three Zig Zag papers and enough to fill them from my father's stash and made the joints myself. They were thin and twisted and uneven, and looked quite amateurish compared to regular cigarettes, or even to the ones my father made. Practice was undoubtedly important. I put them out on the coffee table, which was so covered with rings left by hundreds of glasses over the years that it looked like a design. We watched the joints as if we expected them to do tricks. This was perilous ground and even Fran and Mary had become subdued. I thought about my chromosomes and hoped once wouldn't hurt them.

52

Then Fran, always bold, took one and lit it.

I thought of an old Bob Newhart record I'd heard once where Sir Walter Raleigh calls the head of the West Indies Company in London to tell him about tobacco and the guy says, "Let me get this straight, Walt—you put the leaves in a pipe and you set fire to them?" It *is* ridiculous when you think about it.

We knew that with pot you were supposed to suck the smoke into your lungs and hold it as long as possible for the maximum effect. Fran sucked and gulped on the cigarette, burst into a fit of coughing, and dropped it on the floor. I scrambled to retrieve it while Mary pounded Fran on the back. I stuck it in my mouth and inhaled. The smoke was hot and bitter and hurt all the way down. My lungs felt scraped, but I held it as long as I could before the need to cough became irresistible. This time *I* dropped it while I coughed. And coughed and coughed. Mary picked it up, inhaled as if she were taking medicine, held it, blew it out, and passed it to Fran, without saying a word and without coughing.

"We shouldn't be doing this," I said.

"Don't," Mary said. She was sitting on the floor with her back against the couch and she reached her arm over my knees and hugged them. "Everything's all right. This is just an experiment. And there's three of us. We won't let anything happen. We take care of each other. We always have. There's nothing more important than that, right?"

"Right," I said sadly, taking the cigarette from Fran and inhaling again. Something funny was happening to my eyes. They seemed to be focusing in a different way.

"Right," Fran said, passing me the saucer we were using as an ashtray.

·   ·   ·

We finished the reefer and lit another one. I slid over on the couch until I was lying on my back blowing smoke at the ceiling. Fran sat on the floor facing Mary across the coffee table. The music throbbed around us.

I have always wished there was a ceremony to mark the passage from childhood to adulthood. I realize it doesn't really happen at a certain age or overnight, but maybe, if the ceremony was impressive enough, people would try a little harder afterward to act grown-up. I know about bar mitzvahs, but I think thirteen is too soon. The ones I like best, that seem significant enough to me, are the American Indian ones that involve fasting, going out on your own in the wilderness, killing bears, staring into the sun, being tattooed. Something you would *remember*. Something that would make you *feel* grown-up. If my father had had one of those, maybe he'd have been more of a real father. Maybe what we were trying to do that night was to make our own coming-of-age ceremony.

"I don't want to smoke any more of that stuff," I said when we'd finished the second joint. "You two can have the last one." My eyes were struggling to keep from crossing and I didn't like the sensation.

"I don't want it," Fran said. "My throat's sore from the smoke already. I've had enough to know what it's like."

"Well, I can't smoke it by myself," Mary said. "I don't want to, anyway."

"I'll take it apart, then, and put it back in my father's box."

"How do we feel?" Fran asked.

"Cross-eyed," I said. "And sad."

"Mellow," Mary said. "What about you?"

"Argumentative," Fran answered.

"You're always argumentative," I said. "Is this an experience we wish to repeat?"

54

"Maybe," Mary said.

"Really?" I asked.

"It's nice to be so loose," Mary said. "It's probably dangerous for me because of my sugar, but I like it."

"You like it because you're always in so much more control than the rest of us," Fran said. "You have to be."

"You're so right," Mary said. "Therefore, it's not a good idea for me to mess around with things that could make me forget my control. But for a short while, to be free is wonderful."

"Do you need anything now?" I asked, suddenly worried. "Orange juice? Life Savers?"

Mary laughed. "I'm okay. But I've really got the munchies. I'm starving."

"Me, too," I said. "I was too nervous to eat any dinner before you came."

"Wait," Fran said. "Doesn't anybody want to know what I think about the experience?"

"Oh, yes," Mary said with elaborate courtesy, "won't you please tell us," knowing full well that no force in the universe could keep Fran from doing so once she decided she wanted to.

"Gladly. I like it but I also like to be in charge of my own person and my own destiny and I think this could make it hard for me to be in charge, if I did it habitually. However, I'm glad I tried it. I like to be informed." She paused and then said, "What about you, Kitty?"

"It scares me. I'm scared about my chromosomes. I'm scared of getting arrested. I'm scared of getting addicted. I'm scared of getting cross-eyed. I'm too chicken to smoke dope."

"I'm scared of starving to death," Mary said. "Is there anything to eat here?"

I tried to get up from the floor. "I could eat a cow. Whole.

I did lay in something besides Doreen's tofu and ginseng and the usual tired veggies."

"Refried beans and mushrooms?" Fran asked; she knew my eating habits.

"I have some if you want that," I said, still trying to get up. "But I also have stuff for salad and some chips and dips. And there's probably some other things around, too."

Somebody knocked on the door.

7

We looked at one another in terror. Was this a raid? The evidence was gone but the aroma remained and the air was blue with smoke. The knock came again.

I finally managed to get up and go toward the door. Fran grabbed a magazine and began futilely fanning the air, while Mary turned the radio down. I tried to straighten my rumpled clothes and hair.

I opened the door a crack. "Yes?" I asked tremulously.

A skinny boy in an ANTONIO'S PIZZA T-shirt stood there cracking his gum and holding a pizza box.

"You Kitty?" he asked around the gum.

I nodded.

"This is for you, then," and he handed me the box. It was hot.

"I didn't order a pizza."

He pulled a greasy piece of paper from his back pocket and frowned at it. "This is the address. You're Kitty, right?"

"Yes, but I . . ."

He interrupted me. "Nick ordered this thirty minutes ago. I brought it as soon as it was out of the oven."

"Nick ordered this?"

"Yeah. It says here: 'Ordered by Nick. Deliver to Kitty.' "

"Okay. Thanks." I backed into the loft and kicked the door shut. Then I pressed my back against it and slid down to sit on the floor. "My knees are knocking so much I can't stand up," I said. "I thought we'd had it."

"Pizza?" Fran asked.

Mary lifted the lid. It was Antonio's Special—a giant pizza with everything. "Where did this come from?" she asked.

"It's from Nick," I said. "The delivery boy said Nick ordered it. Mary, did you tell him what we were doing tonight?"

"No," Mary said, sitting back on her heels. "Just that we were all staying here tonight. Wasn't that sweet of him? And just in time, too."

Sitting on the floor by the door, we fell on the pizza like a pack of vultures. Nick, the dream boyfriend, I thought. Not only was he thinking of Mary's pleasure, even when he wasn't with her, he was thinking of her friends, too. He should be giving lessons to every other boy in school.

When we finished the pizza, we figured enough time had passed so we could safely start drinking.

Fran had brought her thesaurus because she said there were so many funny words in it for drunkards she thought we should each pick one for our very own to get into the proper frame of mind. I debated between "tippler" and "sponge" and then chose "tippler." It seemed more genteel. Though I don't know why I was worried about being genteel when my aim was to get "blitzed" ("hammered," "stinko," "shellacked," "soaked," "boiled," "fried," and/or "canned"). Mary picked "tosspot" and Fran was "Admiral of the Red."

Even funnier were some of the names for intoxicating spirits. My personal favorite is "nose paint," but I also like "neck oil," "corpse reviver," "popskull," and "coffin varnish." While we were at it, I looked up words for cigarettes; there were only a few, the best of which was "gasper." And for dope there were even fewer, except for the different street names for the various drugs. It made me wonder if the more attractive the vice is, the more nicknames it has. If that was the case, we were in for a real treat when we started drinking.

"Well, Admiral, pour me a little snort of nose paint," I said.

Fran gave us each a half inch of vodka to begin with and we poured it down our throats. It seemed more efficient to do it that way than to sip at it and prolong the agony. I could feel it all the way down. When it hit my stomach, it was almost as if it were digging a hole in it.

"God!" I yelled, reaching for one of the glasses of water Fran had arranged on the coffee table. "Ow!" Then I was aware of little warm tendrils reaching out from the hot spot in my stomach, a very odd sensation. There was still a medicinal taste in my mouth.

Next Fran poured us each a half inch of Scotch. Talk about a medicinal taste! But the warm feeling in my stomach grew when the Scotch joined the vodka. It didn't hurt as much this time, either. We sat warily, waiting for something to happen, but all we felt was wary.

A half inch of bourbon followed a half inch of gin. For some reason Fran thought it was aesthetically pleasing to our stomachs to have clear booze followed by darker booze. I swallowed everything so fast I could barely tell how it tasted. But then,

I guess the reason I was swallowing so fast was that it tasted so bad.

After two inches we thought it wise to stop for a little while and see what happened. My eyes felt crossed again.

"I don't see how people get addicted to this stuff," I said. "It tastes disgusting."

"You ever hear of rum and Coke? Bourbon and ginger ale? Mai-tais and piña coladas and daiquiris?" Fran asked, rearranging the bottles and glasses on the table according to some plan only she understood. "What do you think the mixer is for?"

"It's the same as being addicted to chocolate," Mary said, laying her head down on the table in the midst of Fran's arrangement.

"That's different," I said. "Chocolate tastes marvelous."

"That reminds me of a story," Mary said and, with her head still on the table, launched into a long tale about two competing tribes of pygmies in the jungle who made raids on each other's village in the dead of night. One night one tribe managed to steal the other tribe's throne from their king's hut. They raced back to their village with it and hid it up in the rafters of their biggest thatched hut. They wanted to use it for *their* king. Well, the next day the tribe they stole it from came bashing through the jungle, ready to fight. They demanded their throne back. "We don't have your throne," the thieves said innocently. Just then the throne fell out of the rafters onto their king, killing him. Which just proves that people who live in grass houses shouldn't stow thrones.

That struck me as inordinately funny and I laughed for a long time and then was so weak I couldn't get off the floor. Maybe I was more affected by this carousing than I thought.

"How are we feeling now?" I asked.

"I must say," Fran said, still moving glasses and bottles

60

around, trying to avoid, but not always succeeding, hitting Mary in the head with them, "I don't think I'm affected at all." She swayed gently. "I must be immune to alcohol." She hiccupped.

"I'm sleepy," Mary said. "But every time I close my eyes I get this feeling like I'm being hit in the head. I never heard anybody say that before about drinking. Maybe it's connected with diabetes."

Fran hiccupped and bumped the back of Mary's head with a bottle.

"There it is again," Mary said, and struggled to hold her head up. "What about you, Kitty?"

"I feel cross-eyed and weak, and I don't like it. Being drunk doesn't fit in with the idea I have of myself. I've always been sush a good girl." I sighed. "You'd think, with the kind of parents I have, I wouldn't be that way."

"It's a perfectly—hic—normal contrary reaction," Fran said. "Anyway, after tonight I think you're cured. Hic."

"Do you know I've never even shaid a really bad word."

"Like what?" Mary asked. She was sitting up now, but her chin kept falling to her chest.

"You know. Like sh— or f—, see, I can't do it."

"Those are just words," Fran said. "Arbitrary designations for something—hic—just like all words are. Nothing happens to you if you say them, any more than something happens to you if you—hic—say 'squirrel' or 'fulcrum.' They're just random combinations of letters, made into words which are recognized by most people who speak your language. Hic." She slid gradually to the right until she was leaning against the couch.

The next time I get drunk with Fran, I'll bring earmuffs.

"The only thing that might happen to you, Kitty," Mary said, speaking very slowly and precisely, "is that somebody who

61

is offended by those random combinations of letters might punch you in the nose. You can't deny, Fran, that words are more than arbitrary designations. They have emotional impact and connotative value, too."

Now Mary! What happened to people who want to sing barbershop quartets when they're drunk? I never bargained for etymological philosophy.

"Um, you guys," I said, seeing two of each of them, "who *cares?* I thought people drank to feel good and escape and have fun. Who needs this heavy conversation?"

Fran's glasses had slid down her nose and she peered over them at me. "Kitty," she said archly, "it wouldn't hurt you to make an effort to learn something. Life is—hic—more than swimming and parties, you know. You must develop your mind. It'll be keeping you company the rest of your—hic—life. Do you want to be bored to death?"

"Thanks," I said, fuming. "There's nothing wrong with my mind. It's good company."

"Now, Kitty," Mary said carefully, her head resting on her chest, "Fran didn't mean anything. She worries about you. She's saying these things for your own good."

I struggled to my feet, yelling, "What about Fran's Stainless Steel Rule: Never do anything for somebody's own good? Have you forgotten that?" I sat down suddenly on the edge of the couch and slid off it onto the floor. "Oh, fick! Shut! I mean, shuck. Fit! Dammit, I can't even cuss!" and I rolled over on my stomach and began to cry.

There was a long silence and then Mary started laughing. She lay down next to me on the floor and hugged me. "Kitty," she said, gasping with laughter, "I never heard a better swear word than 'fick.' I love it. That makes a great swear . . ."

Fran reached up onto the couch and took hold of a pillow.

She lobbed it over the coffee table and it fell on Mary and me. Mary, lying next to me on the floor, said, "I'm getting that feeling again, of being hit in the head. But it's different this time."

"It's a pillow, Mary," I said. "Fran threw a pillow at us."

Mary sat up. "Why did you do that?" she asked Fran.

Fran hiccupped and reached for another pillow. She threw it in a high arc over the coffee table and it hit Mary in the chest. She rocked slowly backward until she fell over.

"Hey!" she said, sitting up. She picked the pillow out of her lap and threw it across the table at Fran. It bounced off her shoulder, eliciting a loud hiccup. Mary threw the other pillow at Fran but missed.

Fran jumped to her feet, holding both pillows, and threw them at Mary, who was giggling uncontrollably.

I watched them for a moment, throwing the pillows back and forth, laughing like maniacs, and I felt left out.

I got up carefully, since I was still seeing two of everything, and walked, with elaborate caution, to my bedroom. I took the two pillows from my bed and made my way back to where Mary and Fran, laughing, falling down, and hiccupping, were bopping each other with pillows.

I entered the fray. I don't know how long we kept that pillow fight up. We were all laughing so hard and having so much fun trying to knock each other over—which wasn't hard, considering the condition we were in—that we didn't even think about stopping until our arms got too tired to pick up the pillows. Then we lay on the floor gasping and giggling and watching the feathers float around the room. Fran had finally stopped hiccupping and my vision was beginning to clear up.

"I've got to have something to eat," Mary said. "My blood sugar's getting too low." She got up and went into the little kitchen. When she came back eating a cheese sandwich, she said, "I hate to admit this, but the pillow fight was more fun than the drinking or tripping."

"You're right," Fran said, sitting up. "Well, I confess I did like how smart I was when we were drinking."

"Just an illusion, Frannie," I said. "I'd rather get high on giggling or swimming than on substances." Substance abuse is what they call it at school in the drug-education classes. It covers everything but, like a lot of things that are supposed to be one-size-fits-all, it's not too accurate. There are a lot of substances I'm sure no one ever thought of abusing.

"You've got something there, Kitty," Mary said. "Especially me. When you have something like I do, every day that I feel regular, not even terrific, just regular, is a high. I don't need anything more than that. I try not to think about it too much, but I know the complications that diabetes can lead to and the things that can go wrong. You don't know how many nights I go to sleep wondering if I'll have an insulin reaction during the night and never wake up. Or if I'll go blind or have to have a leg amputated or if I ever dare to have children."

"Oh, Mary!" I said.

"Don't feel sorry for me. It's made me very independent to know I have to take care of myself. But sometimes I can't help resenting the fact that I can *never* forget about it. I'd love to throw away the insulin and needles and test strips for my urine and my blood and quit worrying about keeping everything in balance all the time. Usually I know having to monitor myself constantly probably keeps me healthier than most people who don't need to do that, but once in a while I just get *sick* of it."

Mary had always been so matter-of-fact about the daily details of her diabetes that, even though I knew it must be a nuisance for her, I never really thought about how hard, and even dangerous, it was. When, occasionally, she complained about one of the routine duties she had to perform, I equated it with the bother of remembering to brush my teeth or to do my laundry before I ran out of underwear. But it was different. I wasn't going to die from running out of underwear.

I sat down next to Mary on the couch and put my arms around her. "I love you, Mary," I said.

"I love you, too, Kitty," she said. "I don't know what I'd do without you and Fran."

We cleaned up the pizza debris and Fran hid the leftover bottles in her duffel. Then we spread our sleeping bags out on the floor in the loft in a row and got ready for bed. My bedroom was too small for all of us and it was more fun, anyway, to sleep in the loft. I lowered the long shades almost to the sills of the windows, so just a thin bar of pale light from the street lamp striped the length of the room.

We each had a different bedtime ritual. I put on my T-shirt and washed my face in the kitchen sink. Fran brushed and flossed her teeth, took her vitamins, did thirty sit-ups, and put on sweat pants and a sweat shirt. Then she arranged a box of Kleenex, a glass of water, her watch, a chapstick, and a portable radio next to her sleeping bag and crawled in.

Mary did things with her sugar-testing equipment and her insulin equipment, brushed her hair, slapped some hand lotion on her face, and pulled on a long-sleeved T-shirt that said H$_2$O POLO on the front and ARLINGTON on the back.

"I love your nightie," I said.

She smiled her luscious big smile. "Thank you. From my personal shopper."

Fran turned her radio very low. We had to have music, even

during the night. I turned out the last light and clambered into my bag, which lay between Mary's and Fran's.

"Is this getting serious or what?" I whispered to Mary in the dark.

"It's a little soon for that, don't you think?" Mary asked. Evasively, I thought.

"So he gives his clothes to strangers on the street?"

She laughed. "It's just a loan."

I obviously wasn't going to get anything out of her, and that was odd. We'd always shared everything.

"Funny," Fran said. "I've never thought of any of us with a boyfriend. I guess I imagined us in some kind of TV comedy-drama, young women living together and sharing the ups and downs of their lives. We'd have dates and even occasional involvements, but our first allegiance would always be to each other."

"It's still that way," Mary said. "Nobody's getting married."

"But it's suddenly occurred to me that some of us probably will. It'll ruin everything!"

I laughed. "We can still be friends. We'll be godmothers to each other's children."

"It won't be the same, though," Fran said. "There'll be a *man* in between us. Sex will start clouding things."

"What do you know about *that*?" I asked her.

"Nothing, as you very well know," Fran said. "But I've seen what can happen. Look what happened to JoJo Alford last year. She was so sensible and so much fun and had everything so together until she got mixed up with Billy Bristol. Then she went around looking like she'd been hit over the head with a baseball bat and hanging all over him in public, and the next thing you know she's dropped out of school for *illness*. Morning sickness, from what I heard." Fran snorted. "She let some *man*, some *child* in Billy's case, ruin everything for her."

"She had a choice," Mary said quietly.

"It must be hard," I said, remembering the night after the movies with Casey. What if it had been Nick instead?

"Yes," Mary said. "Very hard."

"Baloney," Fran said tartly. "You just say no."

"I wish I were as sure of everything as you are," I said.

"It's simple. Just take a stand. Then stand on it."

"Maybe reality is different from theory," I suggested hesitantly.

"Right," Mary said. "You don't know how temptable you are until you're tempted. Sometimes you have to bend a principle."

"Why?" I asked. "What would make you bend this principle?"

"Love?" Mary said questioningly.

Fran snorted again. "You mean hormones."

"Oh, Fran," I said, "stop being such a sourpuss." Sometimes it gets a little tiresome the way she insists on *her* way as the *only* way. "Love exists and you know it."

"You're right, though," Mary said. "It's easy to mistake hormones for love. But Kitty's right, too. Love exists."

"How do you tell the difference," I wondered.

"I have no idea," Fran said.

"I've got to have somebody I can talk to about *anything*," I said. "That'll be my test. And somebody who won't try to dominate me. I know I'm easy to dominate, and if somebody can resist that, I guess it's love."

"I have to have somebody who's not put off by my disease," Mary said. "That's basic. Then good sense of humor, kindness, intelligence, generosity, reliability, and a body I can't keep my hands off." She giggled.

So did I. Except for the last item, and maybe even that one for all I knew, it sounded like Nick.

It was late and we drifted into our own thoughts. I could tell when Mary fell asleep. Her breathing got deep and even, and the retainer she had to wear on her teeth when she slept made her breath whistle a little.

Just before I sank totally into sleep, I heard Fran whisper, "Do you know why I act so cynical about love? Because I'm so afraid no one will ever love me. I'm not very lovable."

I was too surprised and too sleepy to respond with anything but a sound I was unable to shape into a word.

In the morning, I wasn't sure if I'd really heard those words or dreamed them.

8

Casey asked me to Homecoming. Mary, of course, was going with Nick.

I asked Casey if he could find somebody to take Fran. He gave me a funny look. "I don't think so," he said. "She's so fierce." That was the perfect word for Fran.

As it turned out, I needn't have worried. T. R. Benjamin, the wing on the water-polo team, and as opinionated as Fran, asked her. Later Casey told me T.R.'d asked four other girls first and they'd each said no. But T.R. loved to dance and he wanted to go, so he kept trying. I was sorry to hear that, but I was glad Fran would be there, too.

Mr. Andrade had given me that Saturday off. He was a graduate of Las Piedras High and he told me to yell a few times for him.

Fran, Mary, and I got dressed in as much red and yellow, our school colors, as we could tolerate and piled into Quasimotor. Nick had wanted to pick Mary up but she told him the three of us had always gone to the Homecoming game together and that she'd meet him there.

There was no hope of our winning the game, but I didn't go to games to watch the play anyhow. I went to see and be seen. I couldn't tell you the score of one football game I've ever been to. As far as I was concerned, the purpose of a football game was to provide an opportunity for socializing not interrupted by going to class.

"I have a joke for you, Kitty," Fran said over the back of the seat to me. "I know how hard it is for you to remember a joke but this one is foolproof, if you'll excuse me for saying so. You can tell it to Casey tonight and I'll bet even he can get it."

"Why do you act like Casey's so thick?" I asked. "He gets jokes."

"I don't know," she said. "I always think big jocks are as muscular between the ears as they are everywhere else."

"Well, Casey's not dumb," I said defensively. "He may be a jock, but he's smart and sensible and understanding."

"Well, well, well," Fran said, and raised her eyebrows.

"It's not like that!" I said, but I blushed, and that made me madder. "Casey and I have been friends since fifth grade."

"I never saw you defend him before."

I didn't understand it either. "Never mind. Tell me the joke."

"Okay. How do you sell a duck to a deaf man?"

"I don't know. How?"

"*You wanna buy a duck?*" she yelled.

For some reason, that joke absolutely broke me up. I laughed until I couldn't sit up straight, and I collapsed on the back seat laughing.

"Give her something to eat to sober her up," Mary said. "I think there's some mints in the glove compartment."

70

Fran opened the glove compartment and our list of good words and bad words fell out. We'd started the list the year before as a diversion while we drove to away swim meets. We tried to add one good word and one bad word per meet and that distracted us from our nervousness.

Fran picked it up and read it over. "We haven't added to the list in quite a while," she said. "Don't you think it's about time?"

"Sure," Mary said. "What word do you want to add?"

"How about 'Nick'?" Fran asked.

Mary smiled. "I'm not sure which place I'd put him in," she said.

"What do you mean?" I asked, pulling myself together and sitting up again. "Good, of course."

"Mostly, I suppose," she said.

"What does that mean?" I asked.

"Maybe it's just that he's so strong," Mary said. "He tries to force things to be the way he wants them. But he means well."

"What does he want?" I asked.

Mary looked embarrassed.

"What do you think he wants?" Fran said. "What does every red-blooded young American male want?"

"What?" I asked again. Sometimes I think they could use my skull for armor on tanks.

Mary blushed.

"Oh," I said. "Well, uh, of course you wouldn't, I mean, that's up to you, I mean, you can . . . oh, God, Mary, I'm sorry. I didn't mean to pry. I'm just not used to thinking of you as somebody's girl. I still think of you as part of us."

"I *am* part of you. I always will be. That doesn't change because of Nick. Things are just a little different now." She smiled, but it seemed like a sad smile.

"Sure you are, Mary. We'll always stick together," I said. "We're glad for you because of Nick. Really, we are."

Mary cleared her throat. "Anyway, what about the list?"

"Read what's on it," I said. "I've forgotten."

"Okay," Fran said. "These are the good words: free, chocolate, popular, shopping, royalty, bikini, tranquil. These are the bad words: ought, finish, preplan, sunburn, calorie, pimple, and vomit. What do you want to add?"

"How about reduce?" I suggested.

"Is that a good word or a bad one?" Mary asked.

"Good, of course."

"Are we talking waistlines or allowances here?" she asked.

"Oh, I see what you mean. Okay, how about date?"

"Are we talking fruit or social engagements?"

"God," Fran said. "Is there nothing simple in this life?"

"Pink?" I asked.

"Color or political persuasion?"

"Gay?" Fran asked wickedly. "Grass? Fairy?"

"Forget it," I said. "How about fleas?"

"I see nothing wrong with that," Mary said. "Anybody?"

"Nope. Okay with me," Fran said, writing it down. "How about 'cash' for the good list?"

"Now you're talking."

We pulled into the parking lot next to the football field. We were early but everybody else was, too, so Mary created a parking place in the grass and we got out. Concessions were set up around the perimeter of the field, manned by the members of other school teams. Mary spotted Nick in the hot-dog booth and said, "Anybody want a hot dog?" Nobody did, but she went over anyway.

I saw Casey in back of the hot-dog booth talking to the water-polo coach. It looked as if they were arguing. Fran wanted to find a seat, so I told her to go ahead and to save room for me. Then Casey went to the nachos stand, talked to one of the boys there who was on the tennis team, and got into the booth. The tennis player left and joined Nick in the hot-dog booth. Nick slapped him on the back and they seemed to be having a great time.

I was so curious I couldn't control myself. I went up to the nachos stand and said, "Hi, Casey." He looked so glad to see me I was embarrassed. I've always wanted somebody to look at me like that, but I didn't think it would be Casey.

"Hi, Kitty! Want some nachos?"

"No. Well, okay." At least I tried to resist eating something I shouldn't. "I thought the water-polo team had hot dogs and the tennis team had nachos."

"I switched."

"How come?"

He handed me the nachos. "I just preferred to work here with my pal . . . what's your name, man?" he asked the other boy in the booth.

"Roger."

"Right. My old pal Roger."

"Aren't you and Nick pals?" I asked.

"We're acquaintances," Casey said.

"Acquaintances! You're more than that, aren't you?"

"Kitty, I'd love to stand here exploring degrees of intimacy with you," he leered, wiggling his eyebrows like Groucho Marx, "but I have important work to do. Dishing up nachos is work for a real man, but I've been training and I think I'm equal to the task. Where are you sitting? I'll join you when my shift is over."

"I don't know. Fran is saving me a seat. Look for me."

"Okay." And he turned away to wait on someone else.

73

Eventually I found Fran, after stopping to talk to a lot of people, and sat down just as the second quarter started. I saw Mary and Nick come into the bleachers and sit below us. Even from behind they looked good.

I couldn't help noticing the way they kept touching each other. They weren't blatant about it, the way JoJo Alford and Billy Bristol had been, but they were *always* touching *somewhere.* Their shoulders leaned together, Nick's hand was on Mary's back, Mary's hand was on Nick's knee, their hands were clasped, their knees pressed together, they were in continuous contact. I sighed.

"What's wrong?" Fran asked. "That sigh came from your heels."

"Oh, nothing."

She followed my eyes. "Oh. Yeah. It sure makes me feel ordinary."

"That's it. I've always had this idea that something big and exciting was just waiting to happen to me. Any day it could arrive for *me,* because I deserve it more than anybody else. I live in a constant state of anticipation. But it never comes. Do you think I could be fooling myself, that I really *am* ordinary and that nothing will ever happen to me?"

"I don't know. Remember the corollary to Fran's Law: Hardly anybody ever gets what she really deserves. Anyway, maybe your wonderful thing will come when you're forty, not now."

"Forty!" I cried. "What good will it do me when I'm so old! I want it now!"

"Can we talk about this later?" she asked. "I want to watch the game." Fran was a real football fan, the kind who kept notes on her program about who did what. It was strange, considering how she felt about water polo, and how she deplored the violence in that game, but she found nothing inconsistent in it at all. Football had to do with strategy and intelligence and dance-like precision, according to Fran, while water polo was wet, disorganized mayhem. She was even able to reconcile the fact that she thought jocks were dumb with the fact that she thought football was a game of intelligence. Fran's mind was capable of such remarkable tricks of rationalization it made me feel positively sluggish.

"I guess so," I said with another sigh.

"Well, how about if we talk about something football-oriented?" she suggested, relenting.

"I don't know about anything football-oriented," I said. "How come there are fullbacks and halfbacks and quarterbacks, but not eighthbacks? Not hunchbacks? They all do a lot of hunching. What's a tight end? They all seem to have . . ."

"Never mind," Fran said, and turned back to the game.

Casey and T.R. came climbing up the bleachers with a box of nachos and hot dogs and squeezed in with us. "Booty," Casey said. "Want some?"

What a silly question.

Halftime arrived and everybody stood up, and Fran and T.R. went off somewhere.

"Casey . . ."

"What?"

"Why didn't you want to work with Nick in the hot-dog booth?"

"Boy, you have a one-track mind!"

"Why?" I persisted.

"What makes you think I didn't want to work with him?"

"Casey! You think I'm stupid?"

"What's that got to do with it?"

"You're evading me."

"Why are you so curious?"

"Casey!" I stamped my foot in frustration.

"Look, Kitty, can we talk about this later? I mean, it's so public here. You never know who might hear. It's not *right* to talk about somebody in public."

Of course Casey was right. I was embarrassed by my curiosity. "Okay, sure, that's fine," I mumbled. "We can talk about it tonight."

For the rest of the game Fran and Casey paid attention and I talked to people and wandered around and waited for the game to be over.

I also kept watching Nick and Mary. Toward the end of the game they were whispering intensely back and forth. I couldn't hear what they were saying, but it looked like an argument to me, the kind of argument you have in public where you try to pretend you aren't arguing. Suddenly Nick jumped up and ran down the bleachers just as the gun went off for the end of the game. We lost, of course.

Mary turned and looked around until she found us. Then she started up, against the hordes of people going down.

"See you about eight-thirty," Casey said to me as he and T.R. headed off, hopping over bleachers and shouldering their way through the crowd.

We intercepted Mary, who looked pensive, and the three of us pushed through the crowds to the car while Fran muttered, "Stupid quarterback . . . passing on fourth and one . . . Where'd we get that coach of ours . . ."

I tucked my arm through Mary's. "Everything okay?" I asked.

She sighed. "Nick's mad. He wanted to drive me home. I told him I had my car and I had to take you and Fran and that

I'd see him tonight. He didn't understand why I wouldn't go with him."

"You could have gone with him. We would have driven Quasimotor home."

"But I didn't *want* to. I wanted to go with you. This is my last Homecoming. You and Fran are special to me. You always will be. I don't know if Nick will be." She looked as if she was going to cry.

"Come on, Mary," I said. "It's okay. You'll see him tonight and you can get everything straight."

"He's so stubborn sometimes."

"Who isn't?"

"And other times he's so sweet and understanding and . . ." She smiled. "Having a serious boyfriend is more complicated than I imagined it would be."

"Well, think of your blood sugar. Don't get upset. It'll work out. And if it doesn't, you still have us."

"Right," she said, and squeezed my arm. In spite of her smile, the glow she'd had when she first started going out with Nick seemed to have dimmed.

"Come *on*," Fran called back to us. "I've got a lot to do. Dinner, bath, iron my dress, plastic surgery."

9

Doreen and my father went off to an art film about how awful modern life is, so I got dressed in a silent, empty loft. I stood in the bathroom trying to avoid blinding myself with the mascara applicator and wondering if my father noticed some of the good things about modern life: indoor plumbing and supermarkets and paint in tubes. He wasn't boiling his own indigo and mixing it with egg yolks to make paint.

Casey was there exactly at eight-thirty. When I opened the door for him I felt as if I'd admitted a stranger. He looked so serious and unfamiliar, all dressed up, the comb tracks still showing in his hair. He held a clear plastic corsage box and I could see pink roses the exact shade of the dress Fran and Mary had helped me pick out.

"Wow," he said softly. "You look fantastic."

He held the corsage box out to me and I fumbled with it until I got it open. We both looked at the flowers, wondering who was supposed to attach them to me. Then I picked them up. "I'll be back in a minute," I said. "I need a mirror."

I stood before the mirror in my bedroom, pricking my fingers, until finally I got the corsage on straight. As I looked at my reflection, flushed and formal, my eyes were suddenly full of tears. It was so unfair that I didn't have a mother to pin on my first corsage. And to take pictures and to fuss over me. I wished I'd dressed at Mary's or at Fran's. Somebody else's mother was better than none at all. I even wished Doreen had stayed home.

I patted a tissue around my eyes, carefully so I wouldn't smear my mascara, and went back to Casey, still waiting by the door. I smiled at him and we went silently and solemnly down the two flights of stairs to the car.

When we got to school the parking lot was full and there were already a lot of people in the gym. It was decorated with red and yellow streamers, making a tent effect. The theme of the dance was "Under the Big Top" and there were clown centerpieces on the tables and lots of balloons. A gym is a gym, though. The band, the Smuckers, was warming up. There was a sign on the drum that said, JAM WITH THE SMUCKERS.

We spotted T.R. and Fran sitting at a table for six and went to join them. Fran wore a severely tailored dress of sapphire blue silk and dangly earrings set with blue stones. She looked more stylish than any other girl in the room and I suddenly quit worrying about her romantic future. Somewhere there was somebody sophisticated enough for her. He just wasn't at Las Piedras High. He was a man and these guys were still boys.

"You look marvelous," I told her.

She smiled. "The plastic surgery was a success."

The band was so loud it was hard to talk, so we danced

instead. Casey was a good and enthusiastic dancer and dancing with him was fun.

By the time the band took a break, I was hot and out of breath from so much exercise. "Let's go outside and cool off," Casey said.

I retrieved my shoes from under the table and we went out onto the track. I shivered at the sudden chill on my hot body. "Cold?" Casey asked.

"A little."

He put his arm around my shoulders. "Better?"

I nodded and we walked slowly around the cinder track. The colored lights from the gym spilled out the open doors, making bright patchwork on the track and the grass. Beyond the reach of the lights, the fields were dark, lit only by stars. Shapes of other couples moved in the shadows.

"I'm having a great time," Casey said.

"Me too. The band's good, even if they do have a dumb name."

"Fran and T.R. seem to be getting along all right, too."

"No fistfights yet. As long as they stay away from politics they'll be okay."

"I haven't seen Mary. Aren't she and Nick coming?"

"They're supposed to be here. I guess they're just late. That reminds me. About the hot-dog booth this afternoon . . ."

He laughed. "Boy, you never give up."

"Well?"

He stopped walking. "Kitty, I hate to say this, but Nick's not somebody I want to spend time with. I know everybody likes him, but there's something odd about him and it's worrying me. I don't have anything concrete, but he gives me an uneasy feeling. He was bragging in the locker room last week about a girl he'd gone with in Arizona, where he lived before he came here; when he broke up with her, she tried to commit suicide. That's not something you should be proud of."

"Maybe that's not the way he meant it," I said. "Maybe you misunderstood."

"You didn't hear him. And you haven't watched him play water polo as much as I have."

"Come on, Casey. Water polo's a rough sport."

"It's the way Nick plays it—not just rough but dirty. You know, everybody expects roughness at water polo. But there's a line you try not to cross. If you're *too* rough you make the other team mad and they take it out on your whole team. Then *your* team is mad at you, too. If it happens too often, your team gets a reputation for dirty play, and we don't want that kind of a reputation."

"If that's happening, isn't the coach aware of it?"

"I think he's getting there. I get to watch a lot since I'm goalie. I see things the others don't because they're involved in playing. Nick's good. He doesn't need to be as rough as he is. I think he likes it. That's what bothers me. I think he likes hurting people."

The music had started again and the other couples had gone inside. Casey and I were alone in the dark, leaning together against a stack of hurdles at the side of the track.

I shivered.

"Still cold?" Casey asked, and he pulled me against him and wrapped both his arms around me. He felt so solid, so warm and comforting, I yielded against him and, without any conscious decision, lifted my face to him. He bent and kissed me, which must have been what I wanted him to do. I had the same reaction I'd had that night in the hallway before my door: my limbs felt hot and liquid, and in all the world, the only thing I wanted to be doing was to be standing on the cinder track

81

kissing Casey. My mouth felt slack and hypersensitive under his and something in the middle of me throbbed. And it was only Casey, my old pal. Not even my Prince Charming. What would it be like with *him*? I leaned back against the hurdles and we kept kissing until Casey broke it off.

"Kitty . . ." he whispered. "We'd better be careful." He tucked my head under his chin and held me. "You have an unusual effect on me."

"You do on me, too," I said. My lips felt swollen and tender. "I never would have imagined you and me acting like this."

"I've always liked you."

"I've always liked you, too," I said, "but not like this."

"Maybe you should start reconsidering."

"Maybe," I said. But I couldn't begin to think of Casey in that dreamy, romantic way I'd thought of Nick and that I thought I should think of a real boyfriend. Casey was my old buddy.

"Maybe we should go back in," Casey said.

"I suppose so," I said, feeling deprived. I wouldn't have minded some more kissing.

We joined Fran and T.R. at the table, and Fran gave me a curious, raised-eyebrows look. So did T.R. Casey blushed.

Just then I saw Nick and Mary come in.

Mary was wearing a red dress with big puffy sleeves, and as she stepped through the doorway she stopped and stared at the dancers. She looked dazed, like a rabbit caught in the head-lights. Nick put his arm around her shoulders and she looked up at him and they stood there for a moment, pressed together, looking at each other with a greedy look, as if each of them was thinking, This is *mine*. It was such a private look I had to turn away. Whatever their differences earlier in the day, they had obviously resolved them.

82

They made their way to our table and sat down. I wondered why they were so late until I noticed that Mary's lips looked the way mine felt.

"Hi, Mary. Hi, Nick," I said. "You're just in time to hear me tell Casey a joke."

"Shoot," Casey said.

"Okay. How do you sell a duck to a blind man?"

I wondered why Fran put her face down on her hands on the table. Casey looked puzzled. "I don't know. How?"

"You say *You wanna buy a duck?*" and I cracked up laughing.

"I don't get it," Casey said. Fran was shaking her head.

"Casey!" I said. "It's perfectly obvious. The guy is blind. So you have to yell at him to sell the duck. There's no trick to it."

"Wouldn't that work better with a deaf man?" Casey asked.

I turned to Fran. "What did I say?"

She shook her head. "You said a *blind* man."

"Oh, God," I groaned. "I feel so *stupid.* You were wrong, Fran. It's not a foolproof joke."

Then Casey laughed, and Fran and T.R. did, too. Mary and Nick just sat there looking at each other as if they hadn't heard a word.

As the evening progressed, I wondered why they had even bothered to come. They danced only with each other, and though they occasionally tried to participate in the conversation, they kept turning back to each other, putting their foreheads together and cutting themselves off from us.

I felt too confused about Nick from what Casey had told me to know what to say to him. I only wanted to watch him, to see if there was anything visible that would give me a clue to him. There wasn't. Just that same handsome face and graceful body.

Fran and I went to the bathroom together. We asked Mary if she wanted to go, too, but Mary just shook her head and smiled and held on to Nick's hand.

Actually, I wanted to tell Fran what Casey had said about Nick, but the bathroom was full of girls primping and there was no opportunity.

When we came back from the bathroom everybody was watching Summer Samuels and her date do a wild dance in the middle of the dance floor. I won't say Summer had the best figure in the school but she unquestionably had the most. If I were her, I'm sure I'd be tired of so many jokes about built-in water wings and not being able to straighten up after tying my shoes and things like that, but she never seemed to mind. And there she was, out there bouncing around like crazy to the vast delight of the boys.

I would love to have a figure like hers, full and voluptuous. I'm only full in places I don't want to be, and the only voluptuous feature I have is my shoulders, from swimming. For some reason, no one ever seems to pay much attention to great shoulders.

After the dance Casey was hungry again, so we arranged to meet T.R. and Fran at Señor Wong's. I wondered how Casey's mother kept enough food in the house for him. She must have had supermarket trucks backing up to her kitchen door every day.

While we were eating, Fran and T.R. got into a disagreement about women's rights, and from then on their evening went downhill. If they could only have avoided politics for one more hour. They were so hotly into their argument they didn't even look at us when we paid our part of the check, said goodnight, and left.

I was apprehensive about being alone with Casey. In spite

of my insistence that we were just old friends, we acted like something more than that whenever we had the opportunity. Maybe he was right; maybe I did need to start reconsidering. Mary's romance with Nick began like a bolt of lightning and that's how I'd always thought it would be with me, but maybe there were other ways for romances to begin. Maybe you could even start with an old buddy.

It was quite late when I finally got home. I was definitely reconsidering.

I hung up my dress, put on my T-shirt, washed my face, brushed my teeth, and went to bed. I put my corsage on the bedside table where I could see it when I woke up. I thought I'd fall instantly to sleep but I was wide awake. I lay with my hands behind my head and stared into the darkness, reflecting on the evening.

I'd had a great time. Casey was fun to be with. He was more than fun. He was comfortable, the way an old friend is; but he was more than that, too. In spite of all my vocabulary building, I couldn't think of the right word for how Casey was. Maybe there wasn't just one word. Nice. Reassuring. Funny. Thoughtful. Even . . . could it be . . . sexy? I smiled in the dark.

Things looked pretty good at the moment. So what if my upbringing was unorthodox. There was no reason for me to feel sad and cheated about having no mother and almost no father. I could survive that as long as I had my friends. Fran and Mary. And Casey, too.

But something kept tugging at the back of my mind, some little blot on the otherwise perfect memory of the evening. The things Casey had said about Nick.

Was Casey overreacting? It seemed that way to me, but Casey was a careful person, neither petty nor a gossip. I trusted his instincts. But I trusted Mary's, too, and she was closer to the source than Casey was.

I hated to think of Mary being hurt if things didn't work out for her and Nick. She deserved good things. She'd already had enough bad ones: being abandoned by her parents, having diabetes.

Well, there was nothing I could do about it, anyway. Whatever happened was between Mary and Nick, and I had to believe that Mary was smart enough to take care of herself.

Finally I was sleepy. Thinking too hard always does that to me. I rolled over and the last thing I saw before I closed my eyes was my corsage of pink rosebuds on the bedside table.

The sound of the phone ringing woke me up the next morning. Doreen pushed my door open a crack and said, "Are you awake? Fran's on the phone."

"Sort of," I said, trying to open my eyes. "Tell her I'll be there in a minute." Trying to wake up before you want to is one of the worst chores in the world, but finally I got my eyes unstuck and staggered to the phone. I sat on a stool at the breakfast bar and propped my head up with one hand while I took the phone in the other.

"H'lo?" I mumbled.

"It's noon," Fran said crisply. "What are you doing?"

"Sleeping."

"Still? What time did you get to bed last night? The dance was over at midnight."

"I don't know. Late. Anyway, you and T.R. were declaring war on each other at quarter to one."

"And I was home and in bed at one-fifteen."

"That's probably why."

"Nonsense. T.R. and I both enjoy a good intellectual debate."

"Well, did you have fun?"

"Yes, I enjoyed it. What about you?"

"I had a great time. A *great* time."

"What's going on with you and Casey, anyhow?"

"I don't know, exactly. More than I thought a couple of days ago."

"I figured. I guess I'm going to be the old maid of the group."

"No, you aren't. You just need someone really special. I think you're going to have to wait for college to find him."

"Oh, sure. And then I'll be waiting to find him in grad school, and then in the business world. Maybe I'll finally stumble over him in the rest home."

"Come on, Fran. It'll happen."

"Oh, I don't care, anyway. A man is not necessary to a satisfactory life."

"That reminds me, how do you think things are with Mary and Nick?"

"From what I can tell, things look fine. Why?"

"I . . . Do you notice anything funny about Nick?"

"Funny? What do you mean?"

"Oh, just anything unusual."

"I don't know what you're talking about. Have *you* noticed anything unusual?"

"Well, no, not exactly."

"Then what are we talking about?"

"Nothing, I guess."

"Kitty, are you okay? Are you sure you're awake?"

"Maybe not. I think I'll go back to bed for a while. I'll talk to you later."

But instead of going back to bed I decided to have something to eat. Doreen had baked some of her dense whole-wheat bread and I toasted a couple of slices and spread them with freshly ground almond butter from the health-food store. Heavenly. I sat at the bar eating and reading the Sunday comics.

"Have a good time last night?" Doreen asked me.

I nodded, chewing.

"I liked your dress."

"Thanks."

"Something on your mind?"

There was. Casey. Casey and me. Casey and Nick. Nick and Mary. "Yes. But I'll figure it out. I don't mean to be rude— it's just too hard to explain to you when you don't know the people involved. But thanks for noticing."

Doreen put her hand on my shoulder and patted it. "Okay. But I'm around if you need to talk. Well, I've got to get over to the library and do some reading. I'll see you later."

I meant it when I thanked her for noticing. I wasn't used to that. My father would *never* have picked up on something so intangible. It was nice to have someone paying attention to me.

10

There was a water-polo game after school on Monday, and Mary and I went. Fran, of course, didn't. She swore she would never again sit through such a spectacle. "Macho showing off disguised as a sport," she called it. I couldn't see how that made it different from football, but she said it was perfectly obvious.

I wanted to know if I could see the same things Casey saw in the way Nick played. It's hard to hide your true self when you're competing full-out. You don't have time to think about what you're going to do or how it will look to somebody else, you just do it. If you really care about fair play and sportsmanship, there are certain things you won't do, no matter how much you want to win. If winning is all that matters, you'll do them. I wanted to see what Nick did.

We were playing Cabrillo High, a team we were closely matched with. Our games with them were always exciting. When the game began, the first thing I noticed was that the level of roughness on both sides was higher than usual, and consequently the number of fouls was greater.

I turned to Mary and said, "I don't remember Cabrillo ever playing this rough before. Have they always?"

"You're right," she said. "They are playing rougher than usual. But so are we."

"Why do you suppose that is?" I asked her.

"I don't know. Maybe because they have a better shot at being All-City this year than they've had for the last couple of years."

"Maybe." But I wondered if our team *was* gaining a reputation for being overly aggressive, as Casey had suggested. What if Nick's rough play had escalated each successive game to a slightly higher level of violence? That kind of news gets around, and the opposition then comes out fighting.

There was a different tone entirely to that game. Usually our team produced a lot of chatter, an enthusiastic exuberance that reflected the way the guys felt about one another and about the game. They looked as if playing polo was fun. At the game with Cabrillo, they played with a grim, silent competence that had nothing to do with fun. It was obvious something had changed not only their style of playing but their attitude as well.

Nick played with a fury that appeared barely under control. He seemed to be everywhere at once, blocking shots, throwing the ball, receiving it, even if it meant almost snatching it from the hands of one of his own teammates. It was as if he wanted to play the entire game, every position, by himself. And he was so good, and responsible for so many goals, I could see why the coach didn't take him out, in spite of the ferocity of his playing. Every time Nick made a personal foul, which was often, and went to sit on the edge of the pool for his thirty-second penalty, the coach would go over and speak to him. But Nick hardly seemed to listen, he was so avidly following the game, not only with his eyes, but with his whole body, leaning and moving as if he could communicate his energy to those still in the water. He was so focused on winning there was no room for anything else.

I could hardly wait for the game to be over. It was awful to watch our team, which had always been so rich in spirit and eagerness, playing so mechanically. Nick's frenzied domination of the game had removed the heart from it.

There were only seconds left and we were ahead 7 to 4, but Nick's fervor had not abated at all. A Cabrillo player threw the ball to a teammate Nick was guarding just as the whistle blew, ending the game. Nick grabbed the ball with his left hand at the same time as he slammed his right elbow into the Cabrillo player's mouth, so hard that the boy's head snapped backward. Then Nick took off toward the goal, in spite of all the whistles blowing, not even noticing that the boy he had hit was sinking under the water, leaving a slick of blood floating behind him from his smashed lips.

Nick hurled the ball into the goal, even though he must have noticed that there was no goalie in it. All the Cabrillo players, and all of ours, too, had gone to the aid of the injured boy. They dragged him to the side of the pool and helped him out, wrapped him in towels, and sat him on a bench. His lips were bleeding a lot, and he had a stunned expression on his face.

I looked at Mary, who had jumped to her feet and was holding her hand to her mouth as if she could feel the boy's pain. Her eyes, of course, were on Nick, who was running the length of the pool to where the group clustered around the boy on the bench. Nick pushed through them and put his hand on the boy's shoulder.

"I'm sorry, man," he said. "It was an accident. I got carried away. I'm really sorry."

The boy just looked at him.

Nick turned to Casey, who was standing, dripping, big and mad, next to the bench the boy sat on. "It was an accident."

"The game was over," Casey said in disgust. "That goal didn't count. It wouldn't have, anyway, because of the personal foul."

"I can't help it. When I play, I give it everything."

"Maybe too much," Casey said. He turned his back on Nick and went over to the captain of the Cabrillo team. He shook his hand and said, "I apologize from my whole team."

The boys began gathering their towels and other gear from around the pool, and the Cabrillo coach helped the injured boy out to the parking lot. I heard him say he thought they'd better get to the emergency room in case he needed stitches.

I looked back at Mary. "Oh, poor Nick," she said. "He must feel awful."

"Poor *Nick?*" I said. "What about the other guy?"

"Poor him, too," she said. "Nick should call him later to see how he is. But Nick's going to be so upset."

"I'm sure," I said.

"He just plays so hard. He can't be halfhearted."

"So I see." I had seen. I had seen an intensity of purpose that was almost uncivilized, and it scared me.

"I'm going to talk to him," Mary said, picking up her books.

"I'll hitch a ride home with Casey or somebody," I said. "You go ahead."

"We'll take you. We said we would."

"That's okay. You'd probably rather be alone, anyway."

"You sure?"

"Yeah."

"Okay." She walked over to where Nick sat by himself on a bench. The shadows were lengthening across the pool and I could see their two silhouettes blend into one as Mary sat down next to him and put her arms around him.

I went out to the parking lot and sat in Casey's car. When he came out, after showering and dressing, it was almost dark.

"Hi," he said. "I'm glad you waited for me." He slid into the driver's seat and took my hand.

"How are you?" I asked him.

"Lousy. I usually feel good when we win, but not this time. We didn't need that last goal. There was no reason for Nick to get so violent about it. I've always been proud to be a member of this team. I don't want to have to start apologizing for it."

"I don't blame you."

"It was just a matter of time until he did something like that," Casey said, still holding my hand. "Every game has gotten rougher and rougher."

"Is that boy going to be okay?"

"I'm sure he's going to need some stitches, so he'll probably have a scar."

"What about Nick?"

"I never saw Coach so mad. As soon as Nick got in the locker room, Coach lit into him, and as far as I know, he's still at it."

"What about the other guys?"

"They're mad, too. About time, I'd say. They've been tolerating Nick's rough stuff because it won us games, but now they're upset about the reputation we've gotten."

"Do you think Nick will be allowed to keep playing?"

"If I were Coach he wouldn't be. But Nick kept saying it was just an accident. And Coach likes to win games. He's determined we'll be All-City again this year. I know we can do it without Nick, but I don't know if Coach does."

"Maybe it *was* an accident."

"Ha!"

"I guess you're right. Come on, Casey. It won't do any good to sit around feeling gloomy. Let me buy you a little something to tide you over until dinner. You want a hamburger? An enchilada? Ice cream? My treat."

He squeezed my hand and started the car. "Good idea. I'd sure rather look at you over a hamburger and a shake than worry about Nick."

"How about some fries, too?" I said. "It's a whole hour until dinner."

When I got home, Doreen and my father were sitting at the breakfast bar eating peanuts—unsalted, of course—and drinking red wine out of glasses monogrammed *aFg*.

"Hi, Kitty," Doreen said. "Where have you been?"

"Water-polo game," I said, grabbing a handful of peanuts. "Any calls?" I discovered peanuts without salt taste like gravel.

"Fran called," Doreen said. "There's a pot of soup on the stove any time you're hungry."

"We're going to our Assertiveness Training class," my father said.

"What kind of soup?"

"Cream of broccoli," Doreen said. "Don't make that face. It's good. Try it."

"Okay. But I think I'll call Fran first."

I threw my books on my bed and the peanuts in the wastebasket and went to sit at the breakfast bar. My father and Doreen went out the door as I dialed Fran's number.

"How was the legal violence?" she asked. One of her maxims is: Water polo is legal violence.

"Violent," I said, and I told her what had happened.

"Why doesn't Casey think it was an accident?"

"That's not exactly what he thinks. He thinks it's the kind of accident that's caused by somebody who doesn't care who gets hurt as long as he gets what he wants."

"Casey thinks Nick's like that?"

"Yes. I don't want to think so, but that's sure how he looked at the game. He looked mean."

"Does Casey have any other reason to think Nick's that way, aside from this game?"

"Well, he says Nick's always played water polo like casualties don't matter as long as he wins. And he said Nick was kind of bragging about a girl he'd gone with who tried to kill herself when he broke up with her."

"Hmmm. Casey's more perceptive than I thought."

"What do you mean? Do you know something about Nick?"

"No. Not exactly. But something happened today . . ."

"What?"

She paused. "Nothing. Just what you told me about the game."

I felt there was more to it than that, but she obviously didn't want to tell me.

"It makes me a little worried," I said. "For Mary. Until now, I was jealous of what she and Nick have. Now I'm not so sure."

"Well, I'm jealous," Fran said, "but not in the way you think. It's not Nick I want. I guess what I'd like to know is that I could feel the way Mary does. I'm jealous of her ability to commit herself so completely to him. I wonder if I could ever do that with anybody. I wonder if I'll ever have the opportunity to find out. But I have a fear I would always reserve a part of myself just for me. That I'd never give over to somebody else."

"What's wrong with that?" I asked.

"It doesn't seem like love. Love is surrender, melting together. I don't think I'm capable of that kind of love."

"Maybe that's not what love is. Anyway, I know you're capable of love. You love me. And you love Mary."

"I mean loving a *man*. That's something different."

"I thought you didn't believe in romantic love, anyway."

"Well, usually I don't. There's not enough evidence to support it. But once in a while, in my weak, unliberated, sappy moments, *I* want a knight on a white horse, too."

"Really?"

"Oh, Kitty, of course! You're hearing my soul now. *Everybody* wants to love and be loved, to be part of a couple. A *good* couple, where everything works right. It's just so rare it might as well be extinct. But when I see Mary looking as if she's found it, I'm jealous of that *feeling,* not of her having that guy."

"Especially if the prince turns out to be a frog."

"Right."

"Maybe he's still okay. Everybody's got character flaws."

"Except that some character flaws, like homicidal tendencies, weigh more than others, like lack of punctuality."

"I don't know how much Nick's weigh."

"Me neither. I just hope they won't be a problem for Mary."

"But she's so smart and she'll notice something bad. Won't she?"

"I think so. I hope so."

"Should we say something to her?"

"I wouldn't."

"Why not?"

"I don't think she'd take it the right way. Some things you

96

have to find out for yourself. Remember the Stainless Steel Rule."

"But what if . . ."

"Let's leave it to Mary for the time being," Fran interrupted me. "But let's stay alert."

"Okay. See you tomorrow."

The broccoli soup wasn't bad at that.

11

We were approaching the end of the swim season. It would be over by Thanksgiving and our daily camaraderie of workouts and meets would be finished. We'd still car-pool, go to school, and play together, but there was something special about workouts: all of us sharing the pain and accomplishment of pushing ourselves against the clock.

Nick and Mary were spending almost all their time together now. They met between classes, and had lunch together. He waited for her after practice and took her home. He came to our meets, even the away ones, and watched her. Mary often seemed to be in a fog, as if she was thinking of something else.

One day when she was driving us home from school—she still honored her twice-a-week car-pool obligation—she sat at a stop sign for so long I finally said, "Hey, what are you waiting for."

"I'm waiting for the light to change," she said.

98

"It's a stop *sign*, not a stoplight," Fran said impatiently. "It's not going to change."

"Oh," Mary said sheepishly, and started through the intersection just as another car came through from the right side. She almost killed us.

"Mary," I asked, after we had gotten our hearts started up again, "is something wrong? You seem so out of it."

"No," she said. "Well, maybe."

"Do you want to talk about it?" I asked. I'd never had to ask before. We'd always told one another anything that was on our minds.

"Oh, it's just, well, the Fosters aren't as warm to Nick as they are to the rest of my friends. I want them to like him and they stand back. I don't know why. He's always polite and pleasant with them."

"Maybe it's just because they know how much you like him," I said. "The nobody's-good-enough-for-my-little-girl syndrome."

"Maybe," she said. "But it bothers me. That reminds me. Mama Bea wants to have a party for us after swim and water-polo season is over. She says she misses seeing everybody. I guess I haven't had people over as much as I used to. How about a party the Saturday night of Thanksgiving vacation? Is anybody going anywhere over that weekend?"

None of us was, so we agreed on it. We stopped at Fran's house first. "Come on in," Fran said.

"Sorry," Mary said. "Nick's coming by after their game. I have to be home."

Fran and I entered her kitchen through the back door. The front door was reserved for company so the white carpet didn't get tracked up. Fran's mother always looked a bit horrified to see me, as if I were going to spit on the floor or carve my initials into the woodwork, but there was always some luscious, woman's-magazine-cover-illustration goodie in the kitchen, like a decorative accessory. That day it was a three-layer chocolate cake that Fran's mother eyed tragically when we came in. She'd probably have preferred to have it bronzed than to see us eat it.

Fran gave her a defiant stare and said, "Can we have some cake or are you saving it for something?"

"Oh, no, I guess not. I suppose it would be all right if you had some." She wiped the counter around the cake with a sponge, then sighed deeply and left the kitchen, unable, apparently, to watch us violate her creation.

Cheerfully, Fran cut us each a huge slab of cake and we sat down at the table with big glasses of milk to go with our hunks of cake.

"I wish Mary'd come, too," I said. "I miss her."

"So do I," Fran said. "I hope you're not going to get as involved with Casey as she is with Nick. I'll never have any company."

"Don't worry. Casey and I are more . . . conservative. Anyway, you're my best friend. I'll always be around to keep you company."

Fran forked up a large bite of cake. "Did you see what Summer Samuels was wearing today?"

"Oh, my God," I said. "I would kill for a body like that."

"Think how she'll look at fifty. Is it worth it?"

"If I had a fairy godmother, that's what I'd ask for," I said. "A real bosom. Cleavage. Curves. Not just on my hips, but where it counts."

"What for?" Fran asked. "It just gets in the way. Breasts have a *function*. They're not just for decoration, you know. As far as their function goes, size is not a factor. Amazons used

100

to cut off one breast so it wouldn't get in the way of their bow string."

"That fashion'll never catch on with me," I said. "Come on, Fran, lay off. I don't want a lecture on standards of feminine beauty. I *know* some societies consider tattoos and nose rings beautiful. I *know* ancient Hawaiians admired women so fat they couldn't walk. I *know* all that. I still want a bosom. Okay?"

"Fine with me. Anyway, Summer needs that body. She doesn't have much else."

"Oh, she's okay."

"She's okay, but she's sure not smart. She's the one who thought the thyroid was in the thigh. She thinks nuclear freeze is a dessert. She'll never be a scholar."

"Never say never," I said automatically. I eyed the chocolate cake and Fran saw me.

"Do you want some more cake?" she asked.

"No. Well, *yes*, but I won't. Anyway, I have to go. I have a lot of homework."

"I'll walk partway with you," Fran said.

I collected my things, and just as we went out the door, Fran's mother came back into the kitchen and ferociously began cleaning up.

"Kitty," Fran asked as we walked, "do you think Mary and Nick are sleeping together?"

"*What?*"

"You heard me. You know people do that sometimes, don't you?" she asked tartly. "I'm sure you've heard about it. Do you think they are?"

"How would I know? What makes you think so?"

"I don't know. Something about the way they look at each

other and touch each other. It reminds me too much of JoJo and Billy."

"But infatuated people act like that. They don't have to be . . . Anyway, I always thought it would make you *look* different, that there'd be some little changes in your features or your posture or something so the people who knew you best would be able to see it and know."

"How about the way she drives?" Fran said. "You know how Mary's always been so independent. She knows what she can do and she knows her limitations, and she's accommodated to them. Why would she suddenly allow someone else to dominate her?"

"I know you have this worry, Fran. And so do I. But he's a dominating personality. He doesn't have to be sleeping with her."

"It's so subtle, so fine, but I see it, I'm sure I do. She wants to please him. She wants to do what he says, even if it's something she wouldn't have done before. Like go to all those water-polo games. And choose activities with him over activities with us. And go out with him even though the Fosters aren't enthusiastic about him—and God knows what in private that we don't know about. Why would she do those things?"

"Your favorite object of contempt: love. Plain old spiritual love," I said. "Well, I'm worried about her, too. She seems so preoccupied lately. She's not as much fun as she used to be. And the way Casey feels about Nick makes me uneasy."

"We have to hang in there with her. We have to be available if she needs us."

"Sure. Of course."

"Any time. Day or night."

"Okay, okay! Here's the halfway point. See you tomorrow."

Fran turned and walked away without looking back.

102

12

Our last swim meet was the Tuesday before Thanksgiving. It was an away meet and Nick was our only spectator, except for a couple of loyal parents who came to everything.

I was the first one finished with my events, so I put on my sweats and sat on a bench by the pool to watch the rest of the meet. I was nostalgic, as I always am at the season's final meet, but more so this time because it was our last meet with Mary. I was so lost in my reminiscences I didn't notice Nick approaching until he sat down next to me, put his arm around me the way he hadn't done in quite a while, and said, "Kitty, my darling, you swam magnificently. A veritable mermaid."

"Thanks," I said. "But I'm glad it's over."

"Let me offer you a prize." From his jacket pocket he pulled a bag of Hershey's kisses, my favorite temptation. He tore it open and handed me three of the little silver-wrapped morsels.

"I *love* these," I said. "How did you know?"

"A little fish told me."

I realized I was starving as I unwrapped a kiss and popped it into my mouth. There is *nothing* as good as that first taste of chocolate when you've really been wanting some. I couldn't even talk to Nick, I was so busy savoring my chocolate. When it was gone, I unwrapped the other two kisses and chewed them up. It's only the first one that has to be lingered over. From then on, quantity is what counts.

Nick held the bag out to me again and I took a couple more. As alcoholics say, "One is too many, a thousand is not enough."

"Now look," Nick said, "Mary's going to swim. I never get tired of watching her." He propped the open bag up on the bench, and while Mary swam, my hand kept going, almost automatically, from the bag to my mouth, and my pocket filled with the little silver pellets I made from the foil.

When Mary finished the five hundred meters I looked down at the bag of kisses and was appalled to find there were only five or six left. I glanced up at Nick to find him looking at me.

"You might as well eat the rest," he said as I grinned sheepishly. He stood up to go over to Mary. "You've got a little chocolate problem," he said. "You better watch it or you'll outgrow your bathing suit."

Something in the way he said that made it sound more threatening than teasing, and instead of continuing to feel sheepish, as I certainly should have, I decided I was humiliated and hurt. How dare he talk to me like that? Then I was angry, but still with that undertone of shame at having my lack of control uncovered in such an embarrassing way.

Nick congratulated Mary with a big hug and then stood at the poolside talking to some of the other girls on the team while Mary went in to shower. I noticed Fran wasn't among the girls he was talking to.

104

I followed Mary into the locker room. As I showered I was acutely conscious of every unnecessary bulge on my body.

Nick took Mary home and Fran took me. As we drove I made vow after silent vow to watch my diet, to eat only things that were good for me, to forswear sweets, at least until I had lost seven pounds. I knew I'd swim faster next season if I were that much lighter. My resolve was absolute.

When I got home I found a note saying my father was at his Aikido class and Doreen had gone to a Dress for Success seminar. I was too full of chocolate to want any dinner so I drank a glass of Doreen's unsweetened apple juice, did my homework, and went to bed.

I lay awake in the dark, wired on Hershey's kisses and anger. Nick was right, of course. Food, especially chocolate, is my weakness and I'll probably be fighting it the rest of my life. Up until that afternoon I'd considered my little skirmishes with calories to be just a part of my life. But Nick had given my weakness a more ominous cast; he had made me feel it was a character defect, a major imperfection, rather than a mere foible.

13

We went over to the Fosters' on the Saturday afternoon after Thanksgiving to help Mary get ready for her party. We'd brought our clothes and were going to dress there, too.

"What are we having to eat?" I asked Mrs. Foster.

"How do turkey sandwiches sound, and cranberry sauce, stuffing casserole, and pumpkin pie with whipped cream for dessert?"

"Really?" I asked joyfully. Our Thanksgiving dinner had been a lentil casserole with mixed vegetables.

Mrs. Foster laughed. "I'm just teasing. I know everybody is sick of Thanksgiving food. We're having a do-it-yourself dinner. Make your own tostadas, and make your own sundaes for dessert. There's a lot of chopping to do for the tostadas, so put on an apron and get busy." She found aprons for us and set us to work around the kitchen.

Mary made guacamole and grated cheese while Fran

106

chopped lettuce and tomatoes and I sliced olives and radishes. They weren't too tempting but I helplessly popped a few of them into my mouth, still suffering from the aftermath of Nick's remark.

Mrs. F. fried tortillas and prepared the meat. The frijoles were in the freezer, made several days before. With all of us working it didn't take long, and then we decorated the living room and the dining room with streamers of red, green, and yellow. A piñata hung from the door frame of the dining room, so you hit your head on it every time you went through the door. We sorted out the best records and tapes, ate a bag of tortilla chips meant for the party, and then went upstairs to get dressed: Mary in a long shift of unbleached muslin, embroidered down the front with bright flowers, and Fran in a khaki skirt and blue button-down shirt. She said she wasn't the type to wear something that looked like a costume, she would feel silly and not enjoy herself, and that's all there was to it. I wore red with a lot of ruffles and a fake rose from the Petrified Florist behind my ear.

By the time we got downstairs T.R. and Casey were sitting in the living room talking to Mr. and Mrs. Foster. Gradually people trickled in, but Nick hadn't arrived yet. Mary kept taking peeks out the front windows. I knew she was looking for him and worrying about him even though she didn't say anything.

When Nick finally did show up, he came in the front door with the biggest, most extravagant bouquet I had ever seen. There must have been six dozen flowers. Mary's mouth dropped open. You could read the envy in the eyes of the girls, and the boys gave each other sidelong looks. Mrs. Foster scurried off to find vases. Mary took Nick by the arm and sort of merged into him. Some kind of background-music tape was playing (what Fran calls elevator music and my father calls supermarket music and I think of as dentist-office music) and Nick pulled Mary against him. Actually it looked as if he *sucked* her into him, and they started to dance, suction-cupped together. The rest of us watched, as if it were a performance. They did look magnificent together, but something about the way they hung on to each other made me think Fran might be right in her suspicions.

Summer Samuels was the last guest to arrive. She wore a dress that looked Tyrolean, with a bodice that laced up from the waist. The laces were loose and it was vividly apparent that she had nothing on underneath. When she came into the living room there was a worshipful silence from the boys before they resumed their conversations.

I danced and talked to people and kept the chips and dips replenished, but I wouldn't eat anything except in the kitchen. I didn't want Nick to see me.

Once, when I was in the kitchen, Casey came in. "You look really great," he said.

"Thanks." I had an almost uncontrollable impulse to throw my arms around him. He seemed so big and solid and safe.

"Can I help?"

"You can take this basket of chips to the living room."

"Not yet."

"Why not?"

"Summer's making a move on me. I'm trying to avoid her."

"Why?"

"Come on, Kitty. She's not my type. She's all brawn and no brain."

"I wouldn't exactly call what she's got brawn."

"Close enough. You're more my type. Some of each."

"How romantic," I said lightly, but I was touched.

"I can be as romantic as you'll let me be."

"I think we've already been as romantic as is a good idea."

"I think it's a very good idea."

From the corner of my eye I saw Summer coming to the kitchen door. And suddenly I was scared to death of losing Casey to her. I yielded to my impulse and put my arms around him. He looked surprised, then vastly pleased, and responded by kissing me enthusiastically, one of those great kisses I enjoyed so much. But this time there was more than the physical sensations I was familiar with. A wave of comfort and connection washed me and I forgot my main motives had been to discourage Summer and to preserve my option with Casey. Was this what Mary felt for Nick? Did feeling like this mean becoming possessed by another person? Did I have to give up *me* to be part of a couple? Could I do that? The comfort remained, but in the span of the kiss, the desire for connection waned. Though I still knew I didn't want somebody else to have Casey. When I was able to focus on the kitchen door again, Summer was gone. And Mary and Fran were there.

"Break it up," Fran said. "We've go to get dinner ready to serve."

"I'll help," Casey said. "What can I do?"

So Mary gave him instructions and he worked with us, while Nick sat in the living room, talking to Summer.

People filled their plates and sat, mostly on the floor, scattered around the living room. I'd been nibbling so much in the kitchen I wasn't hungry, so I changed records and helped serve and pick up empty plates.

Mary went around taking requests for drinks. As she passed Nick he said, "Mary, I forgot my napkin. Would you bring me one?"

"Sure," she said, "just as soon as I get these drinks."

"I need it now," he said.

I looked in Fran's direction and wasn't surprised to find her looking at me.

"In a minute," Mary said.

Nick turned to Summer, who was sitting next to him, and said, "Maybe Summer would share her napkin with me."

She giggled. "Sure," she said, and she tore her napkin in half and made a big production of tucking it into the throat of Nick's shirt, patting his chest, and saying, "I thought Casey had nice muscles, but yours are something else!" She looked at him slyly from the corners of her eyes.

Mary looked astonished. She went out to the kitchen. I followed her and so did Fran. She was holding on to the edge of the sink so hard her knuckles were white.

"The crumb," Fran said. "He's not worth it."

"Don't say that," Mary said.

I put my arms around Mary and said, "I'll take him a napkin."

"No," Mary said. "He wants me to. I'll do it." She took a couple of napkins from a pile on the counter and went back into the living room with them, leaving Fran and me looking at each other.

For the rest of the evening Nick was somewhat less attentive to Mary than he usually was. He didn't stick as close to her and he didn't gaze at her as much. She, on the other hand, could hardly take her eyes off him. She watched every move he made, especially when he was talking to or dancing with one of the other girls. I had the sensation there were invisible lines pulling and being pulled between them, but it was unknown territory to me and I didn't know what was going on.

When Casey helped me carry plates out to the kitchen he

110

said, "Did you catch that business about the napkin with Summer and Nick?"

"You know I did. Mary was upset." I put a pile of paper plates in the trash.

"He did that on purpose," Casey said, salvaging plastic forks I'd thrown away.

"How do you know?"

"I know a power play when I see one."

"Why does he *do* that?"

"I guess some people get off on power. Nick is one of them."

"You scare me when you talk like that."

"Nick scares *me.*"

"What can we do about Mary?"

"I don't know. If she doesn't figure it out for herself, I don't think she'll enjoy having you explain it to her. Maybe she'll have to learn the hard way."

"I don't want that to happen to her."

"You know I believe in looking out for your friends. I just don't know how to do it in this case."

"Neither do I."

When the party was over, Fran and I stayed to help clean up. Nick stayed, too. While the two of us were in the kitchen washing up and putting away the leftovers, we could hear Nick and Mary in the living room. They were speaking softly so we couldn't hear their words, but there was no mistaking the tone of their voices. Nick was speaking forcefully to Mary and she was almost whimpering in response. It made me sick. I wanted to go in there and knock him down.

Fran glared at me. "Do you hear that?"

"I wish I could hear more," I said. "On the other hand, maybe I don't."

"How can he be that way with her? What's there ever to be mad about with Mary?" Fran asked, furiously crushing paper plates into the trash. "I'd like to tell her what I really think about him."

"Why don't you?" I asked, drying plastic forks.

"Remember the Stainless Steel Rule?"

"Oh, yeah. Maybe it doesn't always work."

"Maybe. I'm almost ready to test it."

We finished in the kitchen and made a lot of noise on our way to the living room; enough noise so they would hear us coming and prepare their public faces. When we got to the living room Mary was standing by the fireplace and her eyes were red. Nick was looking out the window with his back to us.

"We're going, Mary. It was a great party." I went to her and hugged her. "See you Monday. Good night, Nick."

Fran said good night, too, and we left.

When I got home I lit two of Doreen's supply of votive candles inscribed *Marcia* and *David* and took them into my bedroom. I put them on the table next to my bed while I undressed. Then I lay down and watched the light flicker over the ceiling. My thoughts were doing the same thing, leaping from one half-formed fragment of an idea to another before I could grasp hold of it. Gradually my mind got out of racing gear and slowed down to a speed where I could think.

And what I thought about was how much I wished I had someone I could talk to about the fears I had for Mary and the doubts I had about Nick and my confusion about what to do. I could tell Fran or Casey my fears and doubts, but they had no more idea of what to do than I did. I needed someone who was older, more experienced, wiser than me or my friends, someone who would welcome me when I had problems to discuss, offer me a safe place to go for help, someone who would guide me into the proper choices and actions and teach me some basic rules for living. I needed something I wasn't going to get: a parent.

My father didn't have what I needed. I thought he'd give it to me if he had it, but he just didn't have it. I needed a grown-up and he was still a 1968-model Haight-Ashbury hippie underneath his job and real-life responsibilities. He wanted to concentrate on himself.

Doreen was okay, but she was only there temporarily. The day she'd gone to that Dress for Success class, I knew her time with us was running out. Her ethnic clothes were being replaced by classics, and she'd given me her necklace of midwife tools.

As much as Fran complained about her parents, she had the kind of bedrock security that came from knowing she had them for allies, and that they would always come to her aid. Mary seemed to have the same kind of thing with the Fosters, but I wondered what being abandoned by her parents had done to her.

Once, she told me she thought it was her diabetes that had caused them to abandon her. They had been married the day they graduated from high school and less than a year later they had a baby and no steady jobs. When they found out their daughter had diabetes, they seemed overwhelmed by the task of caring for her. They couldn't remember when to give her her insulin shots, or how much insulin to give her, or what to do for an insulin reaction. Mary was in and out of the hospital, scared and worried, trying to manage her disease as well as she could, but she was just a little girl. Her parents quarreled and blamed each other, and then Mary, for the complications in their lives; lives already complicated enough by lack of money and lack of organization.

She had been devastated when they had given her up to a foster home.

But now Mary had security with the Fosters. The closest I came to it was with Fran and Mary. And the possibility of losing that terrified me.

They'd found answers for helping themselves. Fran had a rule or a law or a maxim for every possible occasion. Mary had some kind of inner strength. Or I thought she had it. Something was changing with Mary and it scared me.

And I had no answers for me at all; I was too wishy-washy and indecisive. I had only my single maxim: Never say never, which expressed nothing but a kind of bullheaded persistence. That and a few charms like my good-luck medal for swim meets and my daily dose of almonds. Not much help against the tangles and terrors of real life.

I was trying to make up the rules for the game as I played it, and that didn't work very well. I wanted somebody to teach them to me.

I didn't even know what the point of the game was. Winning? Playing? Refereeing? Or just being a spectator?

14

The next few weeks limped along. Close to Christmas the time slows down when you think about how much longer it is before Christmas vacation, but it also speeds up when you think about how much there is to do before Christmas.

My most time-consuming Christmas project, aside from getting through exams, was figuring out the perfect gifts for Mary and Fran. I didn't have to worry about my father. He went into atheistic rampages about Christmas commercialism and complained constantly about the demanding housewives at the supermarket who were never satisfied with the quality of the produce at Christmastime.

"All year they feed their families whatever's there," he ranted. "But at Christmas one little blemish on an apple makes them furious. The oranges aren't orange enough and the lettuce is limp and the onions are too small. What are they doing, giving vegetables as *gifts*?"

I got Doreen a book of famous quotations with her own initials stamped on the cover. I was guessing it would be a goodbye present as well as a Christmas gift. She'd gotten an A in her English class and was working in the registrar's office now instead of as a model. After the holidays she was leaving Brand Names entirely and working more hours at the college. She'd had lunch a couple of times with her English instructor —she described him as a serious handsome bachelor—and once she didn't come home all night. My father seemed angry and preoccupied.

Without swim practice to assure our seeing each other every day, the only time Fran and Mary and I were together was twice a week when Mary drove the car pool. The other days she rode with Nick. Fran and I ate lunch together every day, but Mary ate with Nick.

On the last day of school we finished at noon and planned, as we had the two previous years, to have our annual Christmas luncheon together. I was really looking forward to it, since we had seen so little of Mary lately and I missed the closeness we had been used to before Nick. We planned to exchange our Christmas gifts for each other at lunch, and I was feeling festive, in a high holiday mood.

We went to school decked out in dresses and heels and perfume. After school Fran and I were sitting in the car waiting for Mary when we saw her coming. She wore a navy-blue dress with a white sailor collar and a red bow, and she looked so fresh and pretty. Nick was walking with her, holding her arm and speaking urgently into her ear. She was listening intently and nodding, and then she smiled and put her hand on his face and gazed at him the way a dog does at its master. It made me sick to see Mary mesmerized like that.

116

I said angrily, "Do you suppose we'll ever look at somebody like that?"

"Only if we've had frontal lobotomies," Fran said harshly. "Falling in love is no excuse for checking your brains at the door."

"Are you mad at Mary?" I asked.

"No," Fran said. "I'm surprised at her. I'm mad at *him* for doing whatever it is he does to her to make her so dense when it comes to him. I'll *never* act like that over some . . . some *bozo.*"

"Never say never," I said mournfully.

Mary arrived at the car and got in. "You both look so nice," she said.

We went to Señor Wong's and sat at our favorite back table, where we ordered chop-suey tostadas with fried rice and frijoles. We were silly and giggly through lunch, the way we hadn't been for a long time. It was so good to have Mary to ourselves, without the feeling that Nick was waiting somewhere for her or that she was anxious to rush off to him.

When we finished eating we exchanged Christmas presents. We always gave the other two identical gifts, the way you do with little children, so nobody would be jealous of the other's present. We also tried to give things that were at least partly handmade or somehow personalized. They had more meaning that way, and when you were the kind of friends we were, gifts had to be special.

Fran gave us journals whose covers she had upholstered in calico. She had learned to do calligraphy just so she could inscribe our books with our names and the date and her wish for us to use them to record our most personal thoughts and fondest dreams.

I had made cassette tapes for each of us, compilations of all our favorite songs of the past year: the songs we'd sung on the way to swim meets, the ones that had occupied our minds as we swam our warm-up laps at practice, the ones we'd listened to on my stereo the night of our homemade coming-of-age ceremony. Songs that would forever remind us of the hours we'd spent together during this year of our friendship, and of the things we'd done during those hours. I had spent weeks taping the songs as they came on the radio, or from borrowed records and tapes, getting them in just the right order. I was very proud of myself.

But Mary's gift that year was the most special. She gave each of us a silver heart charm with all our names on one side and on the other *Best Friends*. I almost cried when I opened the little box, since I felt that our days as best friends, at least as we had always been before, were numbered—by Mary's impending graduation if by nothing else.

As we lingered, admiring our presents, Mary asked me what I wanted more than anything for Christmas.

"Oh, nothing much. A set of real parents. A real house. Straight A's. Cleavage. What do you want?" I asked her. "Seems as if you've got what you wanted already."

"There's only one other thing I want and I may get that, too."

"What?"

"I'd like to be cured of diabetes."

"You know there's no cure for that," I said.

"Do you believe in miracles?" Mary asked me.

"Sure. I guess so. Maybe." Decisive as usual.

"Well," Mary said, "things that medical science can't explain happen all the time. I'm sure that as medicine gets more sophisticated and fine-tuned they'll find the reasons for some of these mysterious cures and healings. We just don't know enough right now. But I also believe that some of them are true miracles and there isn't any rational explanation for them. The mind is so powerful, you know. It truly can control your body. You know that from swimming. Your body sometimes does things you swore were impossible for it. You just *push* with your mind and your body responds."

"That's true," I said. "Like those women who can lift up a car when their child is underneath it."

"Right." Mary said. "That's the whole principle of biofeedback, too. You can control your body with your mind. You can lower your blood pressure just by thinking, and you can dilate your eyes and your blood vessels and cause your hands to become warmer. Lots of things."

"You think you can mind-control your pancreas into producing insulin?" Fran asked incredulously.

"I think it's possible," Mary said. "I hope I can do it."

"Mary!" I cried. "Are you serious?"

"Where did you get this idea—as if I didn't know," Fran asked.

"Nick has talked to me about it, but he hasn't talked me into anything," Mary said defensively. "You know how I feel about being a diabetic. I'm good at taking care of myself, but I'd give anything not to have to."

"Do you actually mean you're going to try this?" I asked her.

"Yes," she said. "I'm going to start with small things, like things I've already mentioned, just to see how strong my mind is. If I can control some of my body, I'm going to try it on my pancreas."

I was horrified. What if it didn't work? I didn't understand enough about diabetes to know exactly what would happen, but I didn't imagine it would be anything good.

"Have you talked to the Fosters about this?" I asked her.

119

"No. I want to see if I can do it first, and I don't want to worry them. Promise me you won't say anything to them about it. They wouldn't understand. I hope you do. I wasn't even going to say anything to you, but it just kind of slipped out."

I could see from the expression on Fran's face how she was reacting but that she was trying to control herself. She said, "You intend to do this without a doctor's supervision?"

"I don't think it's necessary. At least not yet."

"You must be out of your mind," Fran said. "That Nick Arlington has bewitched you to the point where you aren't thinking straight."

"Nick has nothing to do with any of this," Mary insisted. "It's my idea."

"*Sure* it is."

"Fran, what's the matter with you? Don't you want me to be cured if it's possible?"

"Of course, but if it is possible, you should do it the safest way, with a doctor's help. Before there was insulin, diabetics used to die. What do you think will happen if you quit taking your insulin?"

"Nothing, I hope. But if something does, I'll start taking it again."

"You know how you are when you're having an insulin reaction. You don't know what you're doing. Somebody has to help you. That's too *little* sugar. I don't know what you're like with too *much* sugar, but probably something similar. If this doesn't work you won't be in any condition to start taking your insulin again without help."

"Fran, I'll be all right. Really. Don't worry."

"When do you intend to do these experiments?"

"Over Christmas vacation. I wanted to have time to concentrate without having to worry about school."

120

Fran and I looked uncertainly at each other and at Mary, who was appealing so desperately for our understanding. We had none. We saw only that what Nick wanted her to do was dangerous. Why couldn't Mary see it, too?

Fran took a deep breath. "Mary," she said, "you know I always speak my mind. I've tried to keep quiet about Nick for your sake, but I can't anymore. Mary, the guy is no good." Mary opened her mouth to speak. "No, let me finish," Fran said. "He's like one of your health-food brownies—he looks like something he isn't. You've changed since you've been with him, and not in a happy way. Nick's not good for you. He's . . . There's something . . ."

"Fran's right," I interrupted, relieved to be able to speak up at last. "Nick doesn't treat you nice enough. And he was only nice to Fran and me until he had you. Then he didn't have to be anymore. Mary, please, get away from him before something awful happens."

Mary looked at me pleadingly. I shook my head. "No," I said. "Nick scares me. He's mean and he manipulates you. *Please*, Mary," I begged her, "please tell him you don't want to see him anymore. Let it be the way it used to be, just the three of us, having fun and looking out for each other."

"I can't believe this," Mary said lightly. "I think you're both jealous of what I have with Nick. You don't want to share me. Well, you won't have to anymore." She stood up, gathered her gifts, and said, "Now it's just the two of you. I'll take the bus home." She rushed from the table.

We called after her, and I got up and followed her to the door, but Mary wouldn't even turn around, and I came back to the table with tears in my eyes. "Did we do the right thing?" I asked Fran.

121

She raised her eyebrows into her bangs. "Take a stand. Then stand on it."

I sat down and wiped my eyes with a napkin. "I kept trying to give him the benefit of the doubt. But he did something to me that made it harder, and then the more I watched him with Mary after that, the more I was uneasy about him."

"What did he do to you?" Fran asked.

I looked down into my lap, where I was turning the silver heart Mary had given me around and around in my fingers. It was dull and smudged by my fingermarks.

I took a deep breath. "I wasn't going to tell anybody about that. It's so vague and so mean and so unflattering to me. But if I can't trust you with it, I can't trust anyone." So I told her about the incident with the Hershey kisses and how I was still fighting the aftereffects of that, still feeling so spineless and weak-willed and resentful. And yet that incident, on the surface, looked so innocent.

We sat in silence for a minute and then Fran said, "You weren't the only one."

"What do you mean?" I asked.

"I didn't want to say anything, for the same reason you didn't—I didn't want to be accused of jealousy, or sour grapes, or imagining things. If only we'd been more open with each other instead of being so afraid of looking bad, we might have headed off this confrontation with Mary. I wonder if he thought of that, and figured we'd be too cowardly to talk to each other about these things. I wouldn't put it past him."

"Fran, what did he *do*?"

She looked down at her plate. "It was at lunchtime one day. In fact, it was the day Nick hurt that Cabrillo boy in the water-polo game. The day we'd gotten back those English tests you had so much trouble with and you'd gone to have lunch

122

with Mr. Roxburgh so he could help you with what you'd missed. So I was eating with T.R. and Casey, and then Mary and Nick joined us. We'd been talking about political activism. Don't ask me how we got on that subject, it was so odd, but T.R. said something about how burning things was a political symbol, like burning bras and draft cards and crosses on people's lawns, and he wondered how come that was. He suggested it was because fire was useful if controlled but destructive when it wasn't, like the wrong kind of political power. I thought the whole conversation was getting pretty farfetched, but you know how T.R. gets off on something and just talks it to death and pretty soon everybody's yawning while he jabbers on. Well, that's what he was doing with this burning business, and the rest of us were glazing over and our minds were wandering, and then Nick pipes up and says has T.R. considered the metaphor of flames of passion; maybe burning things was an indication of the amount of passion invested in an idea.

"And he said how passion for an idea or passion for a person could inflame you in the same sort of way, and the feelings were similar. Mary was keeping quiet and everybody but T.R. was losing interest, finishing their lunches and getting ready to go back to class. So we all got up then, thinking the conversation was over, and Nick says to me, 'I think you'll light a lot of political fires in your life.' Well, that seems harmless, right? I mean, everybody knows I'm interested in politics and maybe I *will* light a few political fires in my life. But the way he said it and the way he *looked* when he said it made it clear that I wasn't going to be lighting any *personal* fires of passion in my life, as if he knew that's something I worry about. Now, nobody else even batted an eye. That remark fit right in with what we'd been talking about. But Nick kept looking at me after he said it, as if he wanted to be sure I got the message. It was the way

123

he kept looking at me that made me sure I'd interpreted what he said the right way. He wanted to be *sure* I knew he thought I wasn't attractive. It was a lousy thing to do and . . . well, it's bothered me ever since."

There was a long silence. "I wondered why you changed your mind," I said. "When I talked to you the day after the Homecoming dance you thought Nick was great. Then a day later you were agreeing with me that something wasn't right about him. It didn't seem like you, to change your mind so fast."

"Well, now you know," Fran said. "You see what he's done, don't you? These incidents—they're exercises of power. He's controlled us by going after our weaknesses. He's hurt us and made us feel fearful and inadequate, and he's done it with just a few words. Really, I have to admire his technique. He's very good. He's obviously studied us enough to know where we're vulnerable, and that's where he's hit us. It's as if he couldn't help himself, he just had to flex his power over us."

I thought about that later and, while I know everybody would like to think her weaknesses are her own special secret, usually they're visible to anybody with open eyes. My eating habits, for example. *Everybody* knew how I ate. One clue was the way I looked in a bathing suit. And Fran worried out loud about being attractive. She just came at it from the opposite direction, always saying how looks shouldn't be that important, and how it would take a special person to love her for herself, and how there probably weren't many people like that, and maybe there weren't even any; covering her future all the time. So Nick didn't have to be a genius to know how to hurt us, he just had to be observant. But the fact that that's what he was looking for is what scared me.

"He's hitting Mary where she's vulnerable, too," I said. "She'd love to be free of diabetes. But *why* does he do that?"

Fran shrugged. "Power is heady. It's a real ego trip, makes him feel superior. Maybe he's compensating for an inferiority complex. Maybe he thinks he's God. Maybe he's a sadist. I don't know. Anyway, what I care about are the results. He's a creep and he's cruel, but in Mary's case he can be dangerous. What are we going to do?"

"Do you think we should tell Mrs. Foster? Mary asked us not to."

"Not yet," Fran said. "Maybe Mary'll wake up and decide not to try it."

"Not likely. Anyway, how will we know if she does?"

"We'll have to keep in touch," Fran said. "After all, in spite of Nick, we still love Mary. And I simply don't believe that she can stay mad at us. But she's probably going to think we're spying on her, under the present circumstances."

"That's true," I said. "But don't you think we have to now that we know what she's planning?"

"You've got a point there," Fran said, "but I don't know how far we can go. Do we tie her up? Squeal on her to the Fosters? Tell Nick we know about the plan and ask him to lay off? We warned her. We told her what we thought. Maybe that's enough."

"Maybe," I said doubtfully. I wished I had someone to ask if it was enough.

In the car, as we drove silently home, each of us wrapped in her own tangled thoughts, I remembered one of Doreen's lunchtime notes: "The only thing necessary for the triumph of evil is for good men to do nothing—Edmund Burke."

15

My luncheon with Mary and Fran had been the high point of my Christmas season for the past two years. My father never did anything about Christmas. I'd heard so many of his Christmas-equals-commercialism lectures I couldn't even listen anymore. Occasionally, the various models had done a little decorating or baking or something, but my father made it plain he didn't like that. Since Doreen was going to see her sister for Christmas, she wouldn't even be around to try anything that year. Her sister had just had a baby and Doreen was excited about being an aunt. I'd promised to feed Onan while she was gone.

As much as I scoffed at Fran's mother and her airs, their house did look wonderful at Christmas, exquisitely decorated and positively baronial. And the Fosters' house always looked homey and old-fashioned, with cinnamon scents in the air. Our place looked the same as usual and I hated it.

The week before Christmas, while most people wrote cards and baked cookies and wrapped gifts and decorated their trees, I slept. Partly from real exhaustion, the cumulative effect of school, and partly to avoid yearning for what I couldn't have.

After great marshaling of nerve, I called Mary a couple of times. I was worried enough about her to take the chance of having her hang up on me. I had the crazy idea I'd be able to tell from the sound of her voice whether her diabetes was under control.

The first time I called she sounded surprised to hear from me, but not angry. She was on her way out with Nick, though, and couldn't talk. She didn't say she'd call me back.

I tried again the next day. I was encouraged by the fact that she hadn't sounded angry the day before.

"Hi, Mary, it's Kitty. Is this a good time for you?"

"Yes, it's fine. How are you?"

"I'm okay. How are *you*?"

"I'm just fine. You ready for Christmas?"

"Well, you know how it is at my house. There isn't much to get ready for."

"That's right. I forgot."

"How about you?"

"Oh, we're busy making cookies and decorating and shopping and all that."

"That's good. Well, I just wanted to see how you were and everything. I hope you have a nice Christmas."

"Thanks, Kitty. You too."

And that was it. Like strangers. I later found Fran had called her, too, but Mrs. Foster had said Mary was busy then and couldn't come to the phone. Fran thought it was probably more wouldn't than couldn't.

I kept worrying. One afternoon when I had been sleeping

and woke feeling especially messy and disturbed, I walked over to Mary's house. It was about four o'clock and already the light was starting to die, the way it does when it gets dark at five. It fitted my mood.

Friendship is such a mysterious thing. Without swimming Fran and Mary and I would probably never have been friends. We wouldn't have had enough contact with each other to know we wanted to be friends. How odd to think that the two people I was closest to in the world could, if they hadn't been swimmers, be walking around somewhere minding their own business and not even knowing my name. Would I have been friends with someone else, then? It seemed impossible. Or would I have been friendless?

Time is what it takes to make a friend. It takes so long to tell each other everything, to make all those invisible attachments of mind and heart, to share enough experiences to have a history together. And there're only a few people it works with. That's why Mary and Fran were so valuable to me.

Wasn't it possible to fall in love with someone and still keep the friends you'd loved before he came along? Is it too life-consuming to keep friendships nourished as well as love? I think, right now, that nothing matters more than the people you care about. Maybe I'll change my mind someday, but what could mean more? Work? Work you love to do must be important and valuable, but whether you have that or not, aren't your friendships still more important? You can always get another job. A friend isn't that easy to replace. I missed Mary.

Mrs. Foster answered the door, and even though Mary had gone to hear the *Messiah* with Nick, she invited me in for Christmas cookies and a cup of tea. I had sat through the *Messiah* once and if it hadn't been for the "Hallelujah Chorus," which got me to my feet, I would have slept through the entire thing. Maybe I'd been too young to appreciate it.

Mrs. Foster and I sat at the kitchen table talking about their Christmas traditions. I loved hearing about them—it was as close as I would get to having any. Then she said, "Kitty, how does Mary seem to you lately?"

"Oh, uh, well," I said hesitantly, "she seems fi . . ." And then I thought, I'm too worried about her to keep it in anymore. "She doesn't seem like her old self and I think it's because of Nick," I blurted. "I don't think he's a good influence on her. I don't know why he has so much power over her, but she doesn't spend much time with Fran and me anymore and she doesn't seem as happy and lighthearted and funny; she seems preoccupied, like her mind is someplace else. All she thinks about is what Nick thinks and what Nick says and what Nick wants her to do. I know some things about Nick that aren't very nice and I'm afraid sometimes, I really am, about what might happen."

Mrs. Foster looked a bit startled at my outburst, but then she said, "Thank goodness. I was beginning to wonder if it was my imagination. He seems like a nice-enough boy, always polite and correct when he's here, but Mary has changed so much since she started dating him, I have to believe he had some part in it. There's something . . . dark about him. I can sense it."

"Oh, yes," I said, and such a current of relief ran through me it almost made me weak. "There is something dark about him. Things happen to people he gets friendly with. And he seems to have a fascination for weakness. I don't know why, but it seems as if he wants to either punish people for being weak or cure them. Make them strong. In water-polo games he picks out the weakest player and is really rough with him, like

129

he's daring him to fight back. If he does, Nick finds somebody else to get rough with. I've wondered if his attraction to Mary has something to do with her diabetes, if he sees it as a weakness."

"Have you tried to talk to Mary about him?"

I told her we had. "She got mad. She told us we were just jealous of her and Nick, and since we felt that way, she didn't want to spend time with us anymore. It was awful. It was at our Christmas luncheon, and neither Fran nor I have seen her since then, though I talked to her on the phone once. Maybe we shouldn't have done it, but . . ." I trailed off. "Anyway, we don't have any hard evidence about Nick, just feelings. It's hard to be persuasive with just feelings."

"Oh, Kitty," Mrs. Foster said, patting my hand across the table, "I wondered why I hadn't seen you girls around here this past week. That just doesn't sound like Mary at all. But I know what you mean. I've tried to talk to her, too. She doesn't want to listen. I think maybe you're right about the weakness, though. Mary told me Nick's mother died when he was born and it seems as if he's always been angry at her for doing that. Mary says he thinks she shouldn't have given up. If she'd just been stronger she wouldn't have left him and his father—as if her death was a *choice* she made. So maybe he does hate weakness and is also attracted to it because of his mother. I don't know. I'm not a psychiatrist and I really don't even care why he's the way he is. I just don't want him messing with Mary."

"I think it's too late," I said. "He's already got her. I don't know what his power is over her and I'm afraid to think about it too much. I remember in history once we were talking about dictators and how some of their subjects actually *liked* being dominated even under bad conditions. Our teacher said that a person could get the most power over somebody who feels both dependent on and affection for the one in power. If those two conditions were met, the dominant person has almost unlimited power. I know Mary has affection for Nick. He made sure of that before he started wielding his power. But why does she depend on him? For what?"

And then I thought of her diabetes. She thought he could cure her. She was depending on him for his strength. Why hadn't she drawn on the strength of our friendship? What did Nick have for her that we didn't? I was afraid Fran knew the answer.

"How are we going to get her away from him?" Mrs. Foster asked.

"I was hoping you'd know."

"We can't talk to her. She won't listen. She wouldn't change schools, not in the middle of her senior year. I don't think talking to him would do any good. What can we do?"

"The best way would be for her to see in him the same things we see. But how can we arrange that?"

We stared into our tea and worried. Both of us, I know, were hoping the problem would somehow resolve itself: that Mary would come to her senses, that Nick would leave town, that she would get interested in somebody else. Yet I knew none of these things would happen.

I took a deep breath. "Has Mary said anything to you about not taking her insulin?"

"What?"

"Nick's persuaded her she can repair her pancreas with biofeedback and she won't be a diabetic anymore."

"My God," Mrs. Foster said, "That could kill her."

"I know. She said on the last day of school that she was thinking of trying it during Christmas vacation when she had

131

time to experiment. She asked us not to say anything to you. She didn't want you to worry. I guess I was hoping she'd change her mind, so I kept quiet, but now I think you should know."

"Thank you, Kitty. You did absolutely the right thing. I'll watch her."

By then it was completely dark, even though it was only about five-thirty. Mrs. Foster offered to drive me home, but I wanted to walk. As with swimming, something about the rhythm of walking makes thinking easier.

I had no guilt about having told Mrs. Foster of Mary's plan to quit taking her insulin, even though Mary had asked me not to. I was relieved to have shared the load with somebody who might be able to help. I told myself it was for Mary's own good. There are exceptions to every rule, surely, even the Stainless Steel Rule. But I was afraid.

I was so afraid that when I got home I asked my father, "What would you do if a friend of yours planned to do something stupid and dangerous? Would you try to stop him?"

"Maybe," my father said, mixing paint. "But I'd be prepared for things to be different between me and my friend after that."

"Why?"

"Because people hate it when you point out to them they're doing something stupid. They never think it is stupid until they go ahead and do it and it turns out that way. Then they feel foolish and are angry at you for knowing they would. Why do you ask?"

"Oh, just curious," I said. He sounded just like Fran. I decided to test Doreen. I went to the bedroom where she was packing. She was leaving that night. I leaned against the door frame and said, "Doreen, can I ask you a question?"

132

"Sure," she said, arranging things in the suitcase, "What is it?"

So I asked her what I'd asked my father.

"That's a tough one," she said. "Certainly your impulse is to protect your friend. That's natural. But what if what appears stupid and dangerous to you is actually just daring and speculative? Adventurous. That's how a lot of great discoveries have been made, by the way. By taking a chance. What if, by your caution and timidity, you prevented someone from making a great discovery?"

"Hmmm," I said uncertainly. "I never thought of that."

"Of course, if you don't stop your friend and it turns out badly, you'd feel terrible and your friend might say, 'Why did you let me do that if you could tell what would happen?' If you *do* stop her you'll never know how it would have turned out. And she might hate you for not letting her find out."

"One of those gray areas, huh?" I said, hoping for some black and white.

"Sorry," Doreen said. "That's life, I'm afraid. As H. L. Mencken said, 'For every human problem there is a solution that is simple, neat and wrong.' "

"Thanks, Doreen," I said sarcastically.

She turned back to her packing, and I went into my bedroom and lay on my bed. My impulse was to go to Mary, tell her everything I knew and suspected and guessed about Nick, and save her from him. Maybe I should have acted on that gut response.

16

Given my father's inclinations, Christmas Eve had never been anything special for us. But that year I was no longer satisfied with meekly accepting his viewpoint. I felt too deprived, especially after the failure of my luncheon with Mary and Fran. At every opportunity I made some remark to him about how empty the season was with no ritual to mark it.

To my surprise, it worked. Right after Doreen left, after he had poured two cups of tea and left them undrunk, smoked a joint while he sat on the couch and stared out the window into the night, picked up his paintbrushes several times and put them down again, he said to me, "All right, we'll do it your way this year. No tree, no presents, no Santa Claus and jingle bells, but I *will* take you out for Christmas Eve dinner."

"You will?" I asked, astonished, and then quickly pressed my advantage. "Someplace nice?"

"Wherever you want to go."

134

"Even the Golden Snail?" I named the fanciest, most expensive restaurant in town.

He sighed. "If that's what you want. But it's overpriced for what you get. It's a rip-off, taking advantage of people's desire for status through things that don't really matter."

"I know, I know," I said, not wanting him to get started, "but I've never been there and I want something special for Christmas. It's irrational. Humor me."

"I *said* okay." And he went into his bedroom and closed the door.

As the door closed I remembered another one of Doreen's quotes, from Oscar Wilde: "In this world there are only two tragedies. One is not getting what one wants, and the other is getting it."

Now that my father and I would be going out to dinner together, what in the world were we going to talk about?

Christmas Eve I dressed in the pink dress I'd worn to Homecoming. My father honored his commitment and wore his one dark suit, with an ascot. As we set out together for the Golden Snail, I made believe we were on our way to a family gathering where we would sing Christmas carols before the fireplace and little children would hang stockings and leave cookies out for Santa.

I know just how I'm going to do Christmas for my own children.

The restaurant was decorated like a Victorian Christmas, with lots of lace and nosegays, a festooned tree, and elaborate floral table centerpieces. It was just what I needed. I ordered a large, rich dinner with a work-of-art pastry for dessert.

My father was quiet, except for a few disparaging remarks about the quality of the Golden Snail's vegetables, and seemed melancholy and introspective. After a while I gave up trying to make conversation and concentrated on the elegant food. Tofu and lentil casseroles just don't taste as good.

After dinner we sat drinking tea and waiting for the check.

"Was that as good as you expected?" my father asked.

"Better," I said. "Some rip-offs are worth it. I wish Doreen was here. I miss her. Do you?"

"I miss *something*," he said, "but I don't know if it's Doreen."

"Maybe it's Christmas."

"Christmas is nothing but commercial claptrap."

"I know. You always say that. But don't you miss sleigh rides and pretty packages and mistletoe and Santa-shaped cookies?"

"I never had any of that to miss."

"Maybe that's why you miss it. I miss it and I never had it, either."

He looked at me thoughtfully for a moment. "It's been hard being my kid, hasn't it? I wonder how things would have worked out if your mother had stayed around."

"I wonder, too," I said softly.

"Maybe I'd have made a better father. Maybe not. I don't feel any older than you, inside. I've always had trouble believing I was somebody's parent. That's been obvious, huh?"

"Yes," I whispered.

"I wish I could promise you I'd be better, but I can't. I know I won't be better. Not unless something big changes in me, something I don't even understand."

"I'll have to take what I can get, then."

"Sorry, kid. I'm trying to find my way, too."

It didn't comfort me to know that my only parent, the person I was most dependent on, not only didn't know how to

136

be an adult but probably wasn't even very interested in learning.

At least he appeared to have some concern for me. That was better than no concern at all, which is the way it sometimes seemed. Thank goodness for Fran and Mary. Maybe only Fran from now on.

When I went to bed that night my stomach was unsettled and jittery. I supposed it was the unaccustomed rich food, and I tossed and punched my pillow for a long time before I fell asleep.

I woke up in the middle of the night to vomit. That word certainly deserved to be on our list of bad words. I thought I would feel better then, but I didn't. I got up several more times before morning, even when there wasn't anything left in my stomach, but I kept trying. I desperately regretted the loss of all that delicious expensive food. By sunrise I was feverish and miserable, and I knew it wasn't caused by rich food. Merry Christmas.

My father looked in on me when he finally got up, decided I had the flu and not food poisoning, and went into the loft to paint all day. He said he'd check on me, but as usual, when he got engrossed in painting, even if it was whiskered old vegetables, he forgot everything else. I walked right by him twice on my way to the kitchen for a cup of tea and he didn't even notice me.

The rest of the day I lay in my bed, dozing and waking, listening to Christmas carols on the radio and to my own internal music, which that day was rock and roll. In a way, I was glad to be sick. An empty Christmas Day is more easily gotten through feverish.

By evening I was better, and my father finally put away his

137

paints and fixed me an omelette, which tasted as good as my rich restaurant dinner of the night before. Then he went out to the corner tavern to have a beer.

As soon as I could get my head up, I had the need to make a phone call, a sure sign I was improving. I called Fran. She had had the flu Christmas Eve day, it turned out, and was almost back to normal by Christmas Day, so clinical evidence indicated I would be okay by the next day. Fran had a well-orchestrated Christmas, as usual, but she said she felt smothered spending the day with her proper parents and her three older brothers and their families.

Then I called Mary. Mrs. Foster said she had been having the same symptoms I had and was sleeping it off. I asked her to have Mary call me when she woke up and meandered back to the living area. I lay on the couch looking at the big dark rectangles of the loft windows and feeling sorry for myself. It was Christmas night, I had no mother, no Christmas tree, no cleavage, and I was alone and sick. Tears puddled in my eyes.

There was a knock on the door and an anger rose in me so hot it almost made me sick again. First my father ignored me all day. Then he left me alone so he could go out drinking, and then, like a child, he forgot his key and wanted me to get up and open the door for him! I pulled my blanket around my king-size T-shirt and stormed to the door.

I yanked it open and there stood Casey with a big white ribbon-tied box.

"Casey! What are you doing here?"

"Merry Christmas. I love your outfit."

I realized I hadn't brushed my hair since the day before and it looked more like mattress stuffing than usual. Combined with my sweat socks, blanket, and T-shirt, I must have looked stunning. "I've been sick."

He shouldered his way in the door. "Go lie down again, then." He followed me to the couch and waited until I'd arranged myself before he sat down with my feet in his lap. "Is it catching?"

"Probably. Fran had it yesterday and Mary has it now, too."

"I'd rather catch it from you than anybody I know."

I laughed. "I must look disgusting."

"Yes, you do," he said. "Luckily I have a strong stomach. And I can see the inner you."

"It probably looks about the same as the outer me."

"Are we feeling a little sorry for ourself?" he asked.

My eyes filled up again and I nodded. He moved up the couch and put his arms around me. "Don't cry, Kitty. You'll be better tomorrow."

"It's not just that," I sobbed, clinging to him. Then I overflowed with my unspent feelings about my father, my mother, Christmas, Mary; everything came surging out in gasping, choking snatches while I hung on to Casey as if he were my only salvation.

He just listened and held me and stroked my messy head. When I finally ran down he continued to hold me. "I don't know what else to do," he said.

Finally I wiped my face with the edge of the blanket and realized I felt like an idiot.

"God, I'm sorry, Casey. That was inexcusable."

"What are friends for? I can't solve any of those problems —maybe they're not even solvable—but at least I can be here with you. Would a little Christmas present cheer you up?"

I nodded, and he put the box in my lap. I undid the ribbon and parted the tissue inside. It was a big stuffed duck.

"You wanna buy a duck?" he yelled.

I laughed almost as hard as I'd been crying a few minutes

139

before. "I love it!" I took it out of the box and tucked it into the blanket with me. "I've always wanted a pet."

"Now I better go so you can sleep. I'll call you tomorrow."

"Good. I want to talk to you some more about Mary, but I'm too tired to get into it now."

"You want me to tuck you in?" he asked. "You're safe from any improper advances because I don't want to catch the flu."

"I'd love it."

He straightened my bed and put a fresh glass of water on the nightstand. Then he sliced an orange he found in the refrigerator and put it in a saucer next to the glass of water. "My mother always leaves us a sliced orange for the night when we're sick. I don't know why, but I usually wake up and eat mine. It seems like good medicine."

"How wonderful to have a mother like that."

"She's okay," he said. "Now get in."

I did. Then he tucked me in, pulling the blanket tight so that I felt encased and safe. He kissed me on the forehead and turned out the light.

I heard the door close when he left. I was tired and light-headed and hollow, whether from the flu or Casey's visit or crying, I didn't know. It was as if I floated in another plane where time was different and abstract thoughts like good and bad and love and fear were almost visible.

I fell asleep without hearing my father come in.

17

I vaguely remember waking up during the night. I ate the orange slices, curled up again, and went back to sleep.

I had a dream about Mary. We were swimming together, and when we got out of the pool and walked to the dressing room wrapped in our towels, something fell onto the deck from under Mary's towel. I stopped and looked at it. It looked like a spark plug. I said, "What's that?" and she said, "It's just my pancreas. I don't need it anymore. As long as I have my brain, I'm okay."

We walked a few more steps and something else fell out from under her towel. She said that was okay, it was just her liver and as long as she had her brain she was all right. A couple of more steps and her spleen fell out, and then her gall bladder and a few more things, and I was getting scared, but she kept saying that everything was okay as long as she had her brain. Just as we stepped through the door into the locker room, two things fell out and Mary stopped walking and just stood there. I looked down and saw a little red satin pillow in the shape of a heart and a small crystal bowl of what looked like cereal mixed with pins and needles. I frowned at it, trying to figure out what it was, until I remembered that the Wizard of Oz had stuffed the scarecrow's head with a mixture of pins, needles, and bran so that he would have bran-new sharp brains.

"Mary!" I cried, "you've checked your brains at the door!" I actually cried out in my sleep and woke myself. I sat up so suddenly my head spun, and I experienced a choking feeling that I thought at first was still the flu. Until I identified it as fear.

Without even trying to figure out why I was so scared, I jumped out of bed and threw my clothes on. I ran down the stairs to the street, and most of the way to Mary's. Whatever was causing my fear was too urgent to wait for a bus.

For some reason I kept thinking of Casey's crippled dog, the one who had gotten run over. If Casey had just started from the porch a moment sooner, if he had only recognized the danger an instant earlier, maybe he could have saved his dog.

I had no idea what time it was. The sky was overcast, and when it's gray like that and the light is so diffused, it's hard to tell if it's 7 a.m. or noon. I only knew I needed to see Mary.

When I got to her house I rang the doorbell and pounded on the door at the same time until Mr. Foster came. He had a robe on over his pajamas so I knew it was early, but he was holding a cup of coffee so I knew he was already up.

"Hi, Kitty," he said. "How are you? Mrs. Foster told me you had the f—"

"How's Mary?" I asked, more loudly than I meant to.

He looked surprised and backed up a step. "Why, she's better, I think. She's still asleep, but I figure she wouldn't be

142

sleeping so well unless she was better. She did a lot of upchucking yesterday, but when I checked on her before I went to bed last night she was sleeping and I didn't hear her get up in the night."

I ran past him into the kitchen, where Mrs. Foster was standing at the stove with an apron on over her robe. "Why, Kitty, what are you doing here so early?" she asked.

"Please go look at Mary," I said. "I had a terrible dream about her last night and I'm worried."

"I know you are but I've been keeping an eye on her and I'm sure she only has the flu. But if it'll rest your mind, let's both go up and look in on her."

I ran up the stairs to Mary's room while the Fosters clumped up behind me. I opened the door and saw her lying asleep in bed. I even looked to see if the covers were going up and down with her breathing, and they were. I was beginning to feel stupid. I tiptoed in, wondering how I was going to explain this to her if she woke up and wanted to know what I was doing in her room at the crack of dawn.

"Mary," I whispered. The Fosters were standing in the doorway watching me. "Mary." I touched her shoulder, and still she slept. I gave her a little shake and she didn't wake up.

I stopped feeling stupid. "Mary! Wake up!" I said, shaking her hard. Nothing happened. Then the Fosters hurried to her bedside and shook her and called her name.

Still, she didn't respond. Mrs. Foster bent down and sniffed Mary's face. I had no idea what she was doing, but she stood up quickly and said, "Burt, call an ambulance. She's in a diabetic coma!"

He ran out of the room and I started to cry. "What can I do, what can I do?" I kept saying. Mrs. Foster put her arms around me and said, "You've already done it. If you hadn't insisted we check on her . . ."

It seemed as if the ambulance was there in a second and the men in white outfits were running up the stairs with a stretcher. It was so peculiar to see those strangers in Mary's room, lifting her out of bed, so limp and pale, like a big doll, and strapping her onto the stretcher. I'd spent a lot of time in that room, changing clothes for a party or listening to records or baring my soul to Fran and Mary. It seemed indecent for a stretcher to be in there.

Mr. Foster had gotten dressed while Mrs. Foster and I waited with Mary for the ambulance, and he rode with Mary to the hospital. Mrs. Foster got dressed then, and she drove me to the hospital with her.

Mary was in intensive care. Nobody could see her but her family, and then only for five minutes out of every hour. I sat with the Fosters for a while, until they told me to go home, that they'd call me when they had any news.

I was so overcome by exhaustion that I had to lean against the wall of the elevator on my way to the hospital lobby. I sat on the bench at the bus stop, resisting the impulse to lie down on it and go to sleep.

When I got home my father was sitting at the breakfast bar drinking cocoa. He didn't even know I was gone. He thought I was still asleep, because my bedroom door was closed. He thought I was sleeping off the flu, the same thing the Fosters had thought about Mary. But Mary's vomiting had been caused by hyperglycemia and diabetic acidosis instead of the flu, the result of her not taking any insulin.

Nobody knew how long she'd been without it. Mrs. Foster had been checking Mary's wastebasket for the disposable syringes that she used for her insulin injections. Each day there had been the proper number of used syringes in the trash. That's why Mrs. Foster was sure Mary had the flu and nothing more dangerous. Mary had been clever enough and devious enough to fool everybody.

Diabetic acidosis results in a sweetish smell on the breath, what diabetics call "tutti-frutti breath," and that's what alerted Mrs. Foster. That was just another indication of how much she cared about Mary, enough to learn about her disease. Even with what she knew about diabetes, and what I knew about Nick, we weren't smart enough, or suspicious enough, or aggressive enough to save her from what I had known, in some deep silent part of my heart, was coming from the day I watched Nick smash the Cabrillo player's face in a water-polo game that was already over.

18

The first few days, Mary was so sick nobody could see her except the Fosters, but Fran and I went to the hospital together, anyway, and sat in the waiting room. It was better than sitting separately at home. Mrs. Foster came out and sat with us when she wasn't with Mary. None of us had much to say, but there was a lot of comfort in being together.

It would be awful to be alone in a crisis. I know each of us is alone, really. Nobody else can grieve for you or suffer for you or endure for you; you have to do it yourself. But the doing is eased by companionship, and I was glad for the company.

Fran and I sat together for hours in that waiting room, but we didn't talk much. Every once in a while Fran would pound on the arm of her chair and say, "That son of a bitch." I didn't have to ask her who she meant.

On the third day Mary could have visitors and we went to see her. She looked awful. She was thin, and her hair was dirty and her face drawn; our beautiful green-eyed Mary. She smiled tremulously at us and I had to struggle not to cry. We hugged her and held her hands and stood speechlessly by her bed. The one thing I wanted to know, and was not brave enough to ask, was whether Nick had contacted her. We guardians of the waiting room had never seen him, but maybe he had called.

Finally I asked, "How are you?"

"Better," Mary said staunchly. "And worse. Stupider."

"Oh, Mary," I said helplessly, "you're not stupid."

She bit her lip and whispered, "That's hard to tell from the way I acted."

"It's all right," I said, wondering what I meant by that. I wasn't sure it would ever again be all right.

While Mary didn't look great, she was infinitely better than the last time I had seen her, the day after Christmas, so I told myself that she would be fine. I wanted so much for that to be so, I pushed back the doubt that flickered on the edges of my mind the way Doreen's candle shadows had flickered on my bedroom ceiling.

Throughout our visit Mary was quiet and preoccupied. Fran told funny stories about Christmas with her stuffy family and I laughed, just as if we were sitting around the Fosters' kitchen having one of our after-school visits, but all Mary could muster was a thin smile. Of course she had been very sick, I told myself. Her eyes were moist and teary, and she kept clutching at our hands like an old lady.

Finally it was time for us to go. Fran kissed Mary goodbye and went out into the hall. When I bent to kiss her she whispered, "It'll never be the same."

"What do you mean, Mary?" I asked her.

"This has changed us. Too much." The flickers of doubt in my mind gathered and grew.

147

"No," I said.

"You were right to doubt Nick," she said. "How could I have been so stupid? He only used me. I was just another experiment."

"Mary," I said, attempting to convince myself as well as her, "he thought he could help you."

"No!" she whispered fiercely. "He just wanted to dominate me. To see if he could break me. You don't know him. He preys on weakness." She paused, holding my hand tightly in both her thin ones, staring past me with brimming eyes. "Why hasn't he called?" she whispered so softly I could hardly hear her.

"Oh, Mary." I had never experienced such helpless pain. I didn't know what to say to her.

She leaned back on her pillow, closed her eyes, and let go of my hand. I stood there for a moment, but she didn't speak, and it seemed as if she was asleep. I kissed her and joined Fran in the hall.

"What kept you?" Fran asked. "Is she okay?"

"I don't know," I said. "Nick hasn't called. Now she thinks he was just using her."

Fran took a deep breath and said, "The son of a . . ."

"Don't," I said miserably. "That won't help."

"Well, what will?" Fran asked furiously when she pried my hand off.

"I don't know," I said. Maybe nothing. Thinking there was a cure for everything was kid stuff, like Fran's rules, which made it seem there was reasonableness to the way the world worked.

I caught a glimmer of what Doreen meant when she said grown-ups take the consequences.

148

19

When Fran and I left the hospital it was getting dark and starting to rain. By the time I got home I was wet and chilled. The loft was cold and empty and the telephone was ringing.

It was Casey. "How's Mary?"

I sat on the barstool, still in my coat, and was warmed just by talking to him, as if more than his voice was able to touch me.

"Sad. Sick. Feeble. Not like Mary at all."

"How's Nick?"

"I don't know. I haven't seen him. He must know about Mary. Word gets around. But he hasn't called her."

"Sounds about right. How are you?"

"Sad, too. And scared. I don't know what to do for Mary. I can see everything falling apart and I don't know how to stop it."

"What's falling apart?"

"Mary and Fran and me. Fran was right with her Stainless Steel Rule."

"Stainless Steel Rule? Anything like the Golden Rule?"

"You know Fran and her rules. The Stainless Steel Rule says don't ever do something for someone's own good."

"Why not?"

"Because, according to Fran, they'll never forgive you for it. And, as much fun as I make of her rules, it looks like she's right. We tried to warn Mary about Nick—for her own good—and she didn't believe us. Now I think she believes us, but she resents us for seeing in him what she didn't." I was so weary, I put my head down on my arm on the breakfast bar.

"Did Mary say that?"

"Sort of. But she didn't have to. You just know things like that. Nobody has to say anything."

"Maybe you should talk to her about it."

"Maybe. I don't know if I can." I was exhausted from worry and fear and sorrow. Talking to Casey was the most soothing thing I'd done in days.

"Kitty, I know I should have asked you sooner—I tried, but you were never home when I called, and I meant to on Christmas but you were so sick and miserable that I forgot."

"Asked me what?"

"Would you go out with me on New Year's Eve?"

My eyes slid open again and I smiled a real smile for the first time since I'd found Mary in her bed the day after Christmas. "I'd love it. A party?"

"There's one we could go to. Or we can just go out to dinner and a movie. Whatever you want."

"I could use a party."

"Okay. Eight-thirty all right?"

"Fine. See you, Casey. And thanks." I hung up the phone

and fell asleep right there on the breakfast bar with my head on my arms. Casey probably wouldn't like to know he had such a soporific effect on me, but it was the most restful and refreshing sleep I'd had in several days.

When I woke up, the room was dark except for the glow from the streetlight, and colder than ever. The rain rattled against the windows, and glitters from the streetlight, captured inside raindrops, ran down the panes.

I turned on lights and heat and brought in the mail. There were two letters from Doreen, one for me and one for my father. I tore mine open.

Dear Kitty,

I can't say I hope you had a nice Christmas because I know how your father is about that. I had a lovely Christmas with my sister. Somehow she's accomplished what I'm still working on —she's escaped her childhood and has made a real life for herself. Her baby is beautiful and her husband is proud and attentive. I want that and I know I'd never have it with your father.

I won't be coming back except to get Onan, but I wanted you to know I'll miss you. When I have a place I'll let you know my number, just in case you ever need somewhere to go. I wish I'd had that when I was your age.

I'm sorry we didn't get to know each other better, but things keep changing. Nothing stays the same forever, I've found.

Love,
Doreen

P.S. I have one more quote for you, from the book you gave me for Christmas.

151

"Anyone, woman or man, who thinks that pain can be avoided inevitably learns that growth, too, has been avoided—Margaret Mead."

I tossed the letter on the coffee table. I wasn't surprised. I'd known Doreen was on her way to something else. She had too much energy to stay with my father for long.

My father came in the door with a sack of vegetables. "Boy, I can't wait until Doreen gets back," he said, "and makes some of her minestrone."

"You better read your mail," I said, and took the bag into the kitchenette while he opened his letter. I leaned against the refrigerator and watched him read it.

He made a surprised sound, then crumpled the letter and went into his bedroom. He didn't come out for the rest of the evening, and when I got up the next morning, he was already gone. It was still raining.

Fran came by for me so we could go to the hospital together.

When we got to Mary's room, there was a sign on her door that said NO VISITORS. We went back to the nurses' station to find out what had happened and were told that she was running a temperature, and because she was so weak, she was susceptible to infection and had to be kept in isolation until the temperature came down.

As we crossed back through the waiting room, the elevator doors down the hall opened and Nick stepped out.

Fran made an odd sound in the back of her throat and we stopped walking. Nick rushed up and put an arm around each of us. His forehead was creased with concern and his eyes were clear and innocent.

"How is she?" he asked. "My dad and I were away for a few days. I just heard."

Maybe it *was* an accident, I thought, looking at his worried expression. Would he really do something to hurt Mary?

Fran moved away from his arm and turned to face him. "How do you think a diabetic who quit taking her insulin would be?" she challenged.

"Is that what happened?" he asked.

"Have you ever heard of biofeedback?" Fran asked.

"Yeah, I've heard of it."

"Well, for some reason she thought biofeedback could help her diabetes."

"I guess it didn't, huh?" Nick said.

"I guess not," Fran answered.

All the time I was just standing there, watching them, with Nick's arm still around me, trying to believe he was sincere, that it was all an unfortunate misunderstanding, an awful accident that was going to have a happy ending. He was that convincing.

"Why didn't you call her or come to see her?" Fran asked.

"I told you. I've been away."

"Didn't you tell Mary you were going? She's been wondering where you were."

"It was a spur-of-the-moment trip. I tried to call her but no one was home."

"You've got an answer for everything, don't you?" Fran said. "Well, I drove by your house the day before yesterday on my way to the post office and I saw you going in the front door. You haven't been anywhere."

Then I, too, moved away from Nick. There was no longer any way I could give him the benefit of the doubt, or try to be fooled by him.

153

"Come on, Fran," I said. "This is a waste of time." I turned to Nick. "It would be best if you left Mary alone now."

"Are you telling me what to do?" Nick asked. The clear innocent look in his eyes had been replaced by something hard and cold.

I took Fran's arm and pulled her toward the elevator, which was just opening. We got in, even though it was going up, and as the door closed, we saw Nick standing in the hall staring after us.

"How can he be like that?" I exploded.

"Maybe he can't tell the difference between lies and truth," Fran said.

"But Mary can. I don't see how she could let him fool her."

"Don't you? If I hadn't seen him with my own eyes the other day I might have believed he'd really been away."

"Yes," I said, "I wanted to think that, too. In spite of everything I know about him, I wanted to believe him, for Mary's sake. I'd rather have us be wrong about him so she wouldn't feel so awful."

The elevator finally made it to the ground floor, and Fran steered me in the direction of the hospital coffee shop.

"No," I said. "I don't even want to be in the same building with Nick. And I don't want to be in the same building as Mary, either, when she can't be with us. Let's go someplace else."

"All right," Fran said.

We went to a doughnut shop across the street from the hospital, but I could only manage a cup of tea.

"Kitty, what's wrong? Mary's going to get better. Have a doughnut."

"No, thanks." I watched the rain hit the parking lot in silver streaks and splashes.

154

"Don't worry. Now that Nick's out of the picture, it'll be just the way it was before with the three of us."

"Remember your Stainless Steel Rule?"

"You don't have to take my rules seriously. I just make them up."

"No, it's true this time. She'll never feel the same about us."

"For God's sake, Kitty, you're worse than the weather. I refuse to agree with you. Mary's not like that. Anyway, I recognize the problem—you have the year-end blues."

"What's that?"

"I get them, too. It's sad to know the year is finished and there's a lot of things you thought, last January 1, would happen to you or that you'd do, that never came to pass. That's quite common. Also, this week is a letdown after the excitement of Christmas."

"Some excitement."

"Even more reason why you're depressed."

"I have to go to work."

"Good. I can't take much more of this. You want to go to a movie tomorrow night? I know it's New Year's Eve, but I have nothing else on."

"Oh, sorry, I'm going out with Casey. We could go on New Year's Day."

"Okay." We paid for our tea and walked out into the rain. "I'll drop you off."

We were very busy at the Petrified Florist, putting together decorations for New Year's parties, and that helped occupy my mind. At five-thirty, after we had gratefully locked the front door, I called the hospital. Mary's condition remained the same.

I went home and made a pot of minestrone from the vegeta-

155

bles my father had brought home the day before, but it didn't taste like Doreen's. I didn't hear my father come in until after I was in bed.

I called the hospital several times the next day but Mary was no better and still couldn't have visitors. Before I left work I called the Fosters and caught Mr. Foster at home. He and Mrs. Foster had been taking turns staying with Mary.

"How's she doing?" I asked him.

"Well, she's pretty sick," he said, "but the doctors are confident they can turn her around."

"How long will it take?"

"Nobody can answer that. It depends on too many things. And Mary doesn't seem to be trying very hard. Of course, she's awfully sick."

"Well," I said, at a loss, "have a happy new year. Tell Mrs. Foster, too." As if sitting in a hospital room on New Year's Eve was an auspicious way to start a new year. "And tell Mary I love her."

Then I went home to get ready for Casey.

My father was sitting on a stool in front of his easel, but when I came in he threw a cover over it. "How's Mary?" he asked.

"The same. Are you starting something new?" I asked, gesturing at the easel.

"Yes," he said. "Something different. I'm not ready to show it yet."

"Okay by me. I'm going to take a bath. I'm going out tonight with Casey Meredith. Remember him?"

"Sure."

I couldn't tell if he really did or not. I took a bath and had a bowl of my inferior minestrone and got dressed. The whole

156

time my father sat on the stool in front of the covered easel. I offered him some soup but he refused. He had turned around on the stool and was staring out the dark windows.

When Casey knocked, my father got up and went to the door. He shook Casey's hand and invited him in. Casey sat, puzzled, on the edge of the shabby couch, while my father made small talk for a few minutes, and then we were released to the party.

"What was that about?" Casey asked, as we clattered down the stairs and went out into the wet street to Casey's car.

"I haven't the faintest idea," I said, and I didn't care. I was so happy to be out of that gloomy loft and away from my gloomy father and my own gloomy thoughts, to be with Casey. I suddenly really wanted to go to a party.

It was a huge fancy party at a hotel, given by friends of Casey's parents. There was food and champagne and music, lights and confetti and balloons. It was wonderful.

Casey and I danced and danced. I couldn't get enough. It was as if I'd been entombed and resurrected; I was grateful to the point of frenzy.

Finally Casey begged me to stop. "I can't keep up with you," he panted.

"Bop till you drop, that's my motto tonight," I said. "I should have known a sissy like you wouldn't be able to take it." We sat for a while, but I had to dance again. Casey gamely tried to keep up.

At midnight I threw myself into his arms and kissed him before he could get his balance. Once I started kissing him, it was almost like the dancing—I couldn't stop.

"Kitty!" he finally said, holding my shoulders and pushing me gently away. "I love this, but it's embarrassing. Do you want to leave?"

"Soon," I said, "but first I want to dance some more and eat some more."

I did, and when we finally left, we sat in Casey's car in the hotel parking lot for a long time. The clarity with which I now saw Nick enabled me to see Casey more clearly, too. I quit comparing him to some impossible romantic ideal and was able to recognize him for the dear, good, rare person he was; a person I was no longer satisfied to regard as my old buddy.

It was very late when I got home, but my father was still on his stool painting.

"What time is it?" he asked when I came in.

"I don't know," I said. "Late."

"Do you always come in so late from a date?"

"Dad, it's New Year's Eve. It's against the law to come home early."

"Is this Casey a nice boy?"

"Of course. I don't go out with anything else. What's wrong with you?"

"I'm your father. I worry about you when you're out."

"Since when? You never even ask me where I'm going. You've always said you treat me like a responsible person because you don't have enough responsibility chromosomes for two of us."

"Well, maybe I was wrong. You're not an adult. Not yet."

I felt decades older than my father. "Are you?"

"No. But maybe it's time I became one. At least time I started thinking about it."

"Why now?"

"Because finally there're some things I want that I can't have unless I'm a grown-up."

"Doreen?"

"Or somebody like Doreen. I'm tired of living like a college student. I'm tired of stacking vegetables. I want a real home, a real job. Work I enjoy."

"High time," I told him, furious that he hadn't decided this sooner. I'd raised myself and the job was almost done. I'd needed a real parent for years, and now that I might get one, it was nearly too late. "I'm going to bed. See if you still think the same way in the morning."

"I will."

20

The next day Mary was still too sick for visitors, so Fran and I went to the movies. We were incomplete without Mary. It should have been the three of us sitting in the dark with our feet up on the backs of the seats in front of us, sharing the good time.

Instead, it was a bad time and each of us was trying to get through it by herself. Fran refused the possibility that things might be different with Mary and us. Mary would get well and then everything would go back to the way it was before, minus Nick. That was how it should be, the Stainless Steel Rule notwithstanding.

I didn't see how that could happen. How could we return to the way things had been, as if there had been no Nick, no Christmas luncheon argument, no biofeedback experiments? All those things had happened. There had been change and there would be consequences.

160

And Mary lay sick and alone, too sick for us to even offer her our silent companionship, too alone to share her misery with us.

The next day, Sunday, was our last day of vacation. Mrs. Foster called to tell us Mary was better and that we could see her for a short while.

She looked much worse than she had the last time we'd seen her, so thin her bones seemed ready to pierce her skin. Pale and listless and dull-eyed.

"I know I look ghastly," she said, "but I'm really better. The fever was terrible; it made me sweat right through my night-gown and I had dreadful scary dreams about dark things trying to get me and I had no place to go." Her voice trailed away and she looked exhausted.

"Let me put you on my Quick Weight Gain Plan," I said. "If you eat everything I do for two weeks, you'll be completely filled out again."

She laughed softly. "I wish I could. Casey dropped in for a minute this morning." She gestured to two pink roses in a thin glass vase on her bedside table. "He brought those. I like them better than that huge bouquet Nick brought to my party."

"Casey's a good guy," I said.

"Yes," Mary said. "You're luckier, and smarter, than me."

"Oh, Mary," I said. "Nick tried to help you." I couldn't believe I was still making excuses for him, still justifying; still, I suppose, trying to make everything be all right.

Mary's eyes filled. "He came to see me," she said.

"What did he say?" I asked.

"Oh, he was very polite. Wanted to know how I was doing and to let me know how sorry he was I'd been sick."

"What did you say?"

"I told him biofeedback techniques don't work for diabetes."

161

"And . . ."

"And he said I must not have done it right. He blamed *me* for the way things turned out."

Before I could say anything she added, "And he's right. If I hadn't been so stupid, such a stupid, blind, vulnerable fool, this wouldn't have happened."

"None of that," Fran said briskly. "When are they turning you out of here? When can you come back to school?"

"Two weeks, maybe," Mary said. "I'm too weak yet to even walk down the hall. It'll be a while. I can have a tutor in here, though, so I'll still graduate."

Mrs. Foster came in then. "I hate to run you girls off," she said, "but Mary needs to rest now. You can come back tonight."

We kissed Mary goodbye. "What are you going to do today?" she asked wistfully.

"I don't know," I said, "but whatever it is, it'd be more fun if you were with us."

A sob escaped from her so violently that she looked as surprised as the rest of us. Mrs. Foster quickly put her arms around our shoulders and ushered us out the door.

We stood in the hall looking at each other. Fran said, "She'll be fine. Naturally it takes a while to get better."

"Sure," I said. "What are you doing today?"

"Oh, God, I have to go with my parents to see my grandmother in the rest home. She doesn't even know who we are, but once a month we go. I hate it. That's not my grandmother lying in that bed, it's some imitation. My cute funny grandmother is already somewhere else."

That was just how I felt about Mary. The real Mary was somewhere else. I hoped she, unlike Fran's grandmother, could return from the lonely place she'd gone to.

162

. . .

Fran and I went back to the hospital that night but Mary was too tired to talk much. She lay on her pillow, holding our hands and smiling at us. We chattered along, but it was uphill work and we were relieved to go.

I told Casey about it later on the phone. "She seems so far away."

"She's been very sick. I don't think that's unusual at all. She'll get better."

"Promise?"

"No. But I hope so."

"Me too. I hate to start back to school without her."

"You and Fran can have lunch with me. I'll pretend I'm Mary."

I laughed. "I always *have* had trouble telling you two apart."

It was strange without Mary at school, but we managed, storing incidents and amusements to take to the hospital for her. We didn't talk about Nick—there wasn't much to tell. We saw little of him at school, and when we did see him, he was alone.

She seemed a little better every day, had more color in her face and more energy. By the end of the week she could walk slowly up and down the hall with us. Her conversation wasn't much, but not much was happening to her. What did she have to talk about?

Mary got stronger all through the next week, and when I went in to see her early Saturday morning before I went to the Petrified Florist, she told me she was going home Sunday and could start back to school on Monday.

"Oh, how wonderful!" I exclaimed, hugging her. "It's been so strange without you."

163

She smiled. "It might seem strange with me."

"What do you mean?"

"Maybe you and Fran have gotten used to doing things without me."

"Mary! We've missed you terribly! Not just since you've been in the hospital, but even before when you and . . ." I trailed off, embarrassed. "Anyway, it'll be wonderful to be together again. We can't wait."

Mary came to school on Monday, but it was an altered Mary, subdued and reticent, almost timid. She was very thin and her clothes hung and bagged on her, like a disguise. Everyone treated her delicately and tentatively, as though testing to see if the old Mary was lurking somewhere inside that loose clothing. There was little sign that she was.

This behavior went on for a couple of weeks. One day, a day Fran was driving, instead of going home after school, she drove to Señor Wong's.

"Why aren't we going home?" Mary asked.

"We need to have a talk," Fran said, and asked for a triple order of chips and salsa, and a pot of tea.

"Okay, now, Mary," she said, "when are you going to start acting like your old self?" I flinched at her directness.

"I'm doing the best I can," Mary said. "But I feel so different now. So stupid and vulnerable. I don't know if I'll ever be my old self."

"Nonsense!" Fran said forcefully. "You're the same person as before. We still love you, and we want things back the way they were."

"So do I. Of course I do. But, Fran, don't you realize that the things that happen to you change you, whether you want them to or not?"

"Certainly I realize that. But you have to put the bad things behind you. Learn from them and go on."

"Oh, Fran, how many tragedies have you had to cope with in your life?"

"Well, none, actually, except for my grandmother being so senile. I don't know if that qualifies as a tragedy. But I know how I'd act in a real tragedy."

"No, you don't," Mary said. "There's no way to predict. I'd never have guessed I'd be so hopeless. And so angry. Angry at you and Kitty, too."

"At us?" I asked, finding my voice. "Why at us?"

"Because you saw what I refused to. How Nick really was. I was too stupid and too sodden with love to acknowledge my suspicions, to even *have* any real suspicions. I thought he loved me and together we'd create a love story better than any one you ever saw in a movie. Love! Maybe you're right, Fran. Maybe there's no such thing. Maybe it's just a disguise for something else—lust, power, control." Mary's voice was hard and there were bitter lines in her face.

"We were just worried about you, Mary. We liked Nick, too. Remember?" I said.

"At first. But you didn't let him delude you the way I did."

"We weren't as close to him," I insisted. "The same thing could have happened to one of us."

"I wonder," Mary said tiredly. "I wish I'd never met him."

I looked at Fran.

Mary went on. "And the scariest part is that I could just as easily do it again. I look back and see what happened and see how it all unfolded and I know that I wouldn't have done anything differently. It wasn't until I was in the hospital waiting and waiting for Nick to call that I figured out what I'd really meant to him. Nothing. Just an opportunity for another experiment."

"Never mind," Fran said stoutly. "Eventually you'd have seen through him, even if you hadn't . . . gotten sick."

"I don't know if I would have. And you two did so easily, along with God knows how many other people. The only solution to this kind of a problem is for me never to get involved with anybody again. If I'm such a poor judge of character that I can't even tell if somebody means me harm or not, it's not safe or smart for me to get close to anybody. *Anybody*," she emphasized.

"But you can't live like that!" I said.

"Watch me," Mary said.

"Maybe you could talk to somebody, a psychiatrist or somebody, to help you," I said desperately.

"Help with what?" Mary asked. "I don't think stupidity responds to counseling. No, I've thought about it, and the smartest thing to do is to avoid involvement. It's foolproof." She smiled bleakly at Fran. "Can we go now? I have a lot of homework."

"Is she serious?" I asked Fran after we'd dropped her off. "Does she mean she doesn't want to be close to us anymore, either?"

"I'm sure she doesn't mean that. She's just upset right now. She'll get better."

I wanted to believe Fran.

The three of us still drove to school together every day, still ate lunch together every day—though now Casey often joined us—still went to the movies together, and talked on the phone, but it was different.

Mary was pleasant and polite and superficial. The three of

166

us had always told one another what we could tell no one else. Now the things Mary said to us could have been said to any stranger on a bus.

Fran continued to believe Mary was healing. "You don't understand, Kitty," she'd say to me. "Mary needs all her energy right now to get completely well, and to keep up with her schoolwork. She wants to go to college in the fall, you know." Fran even made up a new maxim to apply to Mary's situation: You can do only one hard thing at a time. And she often told me, "Time heals all wounds."

Maybe, though I'm not sure about that yet. But I think even healed wounds leave scars.

The winter and spring passed, and we were busy with school and part-time jobs and social things. My social life was shared with Fran and Mary, and with Casey.

My father quit working at the supermarket and took a job at an art-supply store. He teaches kids' drawing classes in the afternoons and is trying to save money. Nobody moved in to replace Doreen. I talk to her on the phone once in a while and she's doing fine.

Most of the seniors, including Mary, were busy with graduation plans.

Each of us had a birthday. When Mary turned eighteen, Fran and I had dinner with her and the Fosters. Mrs. Foster made Mexican food, Mary's favorite, and a beautiful fruit pizza for dessert. When I helped her carry dirty dishes back to the kitchen, she leaned against the sink and asked me, "How long do you think it's going to take her to get over this?"

"I don't know," I said. I didn't tell her what I really thought —that she would never get over it. Along with so much else, my only maxim seemed to have failed me, too. "Fran thinks it'll take a while, and until she gets the whole business about Nick worked out, things won't be the same with the rest of us "

"I hope Fran's right."

"You know Fran. She's *sure* she's right."

Mrs. Foster laughed.

For my birthday my father gave me the portrait of me he'd started New Year's Eve. In the picture I'm sitting at a dressing table before a big mirror. You can see my reflection in the mirror as well as my face looking into the mirror. The face looking into the mirror resembles my school pictures, the way I really look, even to Mary's silver heart around my neck. But the reflection *in* the mirror, while it looks like me, looks different, too: me altered in some way, somehow better. My father said that's how I'll look when I'm finished growing up. He said he knew I'd make it. He wasn't so sure he would, but he was trying.

I hope he's right. The mirror face, even with its suggestion of sadness, looks like someone I'd like to be.

Mary got accepted at Stanford. She told us at lunch the day after she got her acceptance letter, and when I heard the news I screamed and jumped up and down and hugged her. She stood there smiling while I danced around her.

"Congratulations," Fran said, "but I'm not surprised. They'll be lucky to have you."

"Thank you," Mary said calmly.

"Aren't you excited?" I shrieked as Casey tried to get me to calm down. "Aren't you thrilled?"

"Yes," she said, "I'm very excited," but the most she sounded was vaguely interested. Her emotions, since Christmas, seemed muted and pale, as if she was trying to remember how it felt to experience them.

We heard through the grapevine that Nick would be going East to college, but no one knew exactly where and no one wanted to speak to him to find out. I saw him once in a while walking to class or eating lunch with a little blond freshman girl. Mary never uttered his name.

On the last day of classes the three of us had always gone to the beach together to celebrate our release for the summer. It was the same kind of tradition as our Christmas luncheon. I'd been afraid to mention it, afraid that Mary wouldn't want to do it that year. But she brought it up.

"The school year's not officially over without a trip to the beach," she said. "We have to go. One last time."

So, while everybody else threw their books in the air and made confetti of their class notes and ran up and down the halls yelling, Fran, Mary, and I raced for the parking lot, jumped into Quasimotor, and took off for the beach.

It wasn't a great beach day. It was too cool and windy. The beach was speckled with a few hardy people and there was a rip current—easily seen because of the sand it churned up from the bottom—running straight out into the ocean.

But nothing was going to stop us. We changed into our suits in the dank, doorless bathroom, and then, holding hands, we ran, shivering and giggling, into the water.

At first it seemed cold enough to stop our breathing, but after a few minutes of flailing and splashing and trying not to swallow any salt water, we were warm. We ducked under the waves and body-surfed onto the beach. We opened our eyes under water, even though it stung, to have our first glimpse of summer in the glowing green tide. We stood on our hands in

169

the shallow waves and collapsed against each other when the surf hit us.

It was almost the way it used to be, the three of us together, having fun. Then, as Fran and I crouched in the shallows, keeping our shoulders under water for warmth, Mary backed into the rip current and it pulled her away from us. She looked surprised but not scared. It wasn't the first time she'd been in one, growing up in a California beach town, and she knew what to do. Struggling was useless and exhausting, and anybody who knows about rips doesn't waste any time on that.

Mary did the smart thing, as we would expect. She turned parallel to the beach, and as the current continued to carry her away from us, she began to swim with her familiar smooth stroke. She kept it up, crossing the current, as it flowed out and began to weaken, and then she was free of it.

The force of the current and of her resistance to it had carried her far down the beach from us, and Fran and I watched as she swam back to the shore.